Griffin's Storm
(Book Three: Water)

Darby Karchut

Copper Square Studios

Griffin's Storm
(Book Three: Water)

Copyright © 2012 Darby Karchut

Copper Square Studios
Colorado Springs, Colorado

First Edition, December 2012

Library of Congress Control Number: 2012919788

Karchut, Darby.
    Griffin's storm / by Darby Karchut – 1st ed.
        p. 268   22 cm.
    Summary: Having regained his powers, apprentice teen angel Griffin finds himself in the eye of the storm when an ancient racial hatred is set loose, jeopardizing the very existence of the Terrae Angeli and forcing Griffin and his beloved Mentor to battle for their lives.
ISBN: 978-0-9741145-5-2 (trade pbk. : alk. paper)
ISBN: pending for e-book
[1. Angels--Fiction. 2. Apprentices--Fiction. 3. Supernatural--Fiction. 4. Fantasy--Fiction]
Title.
        PZ
        [Fic]—dc22

The author acknowledges the copyrighted or trademarked status and trademark owners of the following wordmarks mentioned in this fiction: Oxford University, Batman and Robin, West Side Story, Saab, Jeep, Velcro, Secret Service, NORAD, John Denver, Wheaties, Boy Scouts of America, Star Wars, Orphan Boy Mine, Zippo, Tinkerbelle, Gotta' Inkling Tattoos

Printed in the United States of America

praise for

Griffin Rising
Book One: Earth
(Twilight Times Books)

2012 Gold Medal—Children's Literary Classics
2011 Sharp Writ Book of the Year
2011 Readers Favorite Honor Book

"Five stars!" -- *TeensReadToo*

"…can't wait to read the next one!"
-- *Readers View for Teens*

"This is the perfect book for anyone who believes that guardian angels really do exist."
-- *National Children's Books Examiner*

Griffin's Fire
Book Two: Fire
(Twilight Times Books)

2012 Readers Favorite Bronze Award

"Recommended."
-- *Midwest Book Reviews*

"Karchut does a good job with her teen-friendly prose and her voice is fresh and engaging."
--*American Chronicle*

Other books by Darby Karchut:

Finn Finnegan (March 2013 - Spencer Hill Press)
Gideon's Spear (February 2014 - Spencer Hill Press)
Money and Teens (September 2012 - Copper Square)

To Wes,
thanks for sticking with me through the Storm

Of all spiritual beings, Angels are most sublime. As far as the heavens are above the earth, Angels are above all other spirits. They are reflections of the Divine Thinker and exist to do His bidding alone. As Messengers and Warriors, they are peerless. Nine choirs there are of Angels: Seraphim, Cherubim, Thrones, the Virtues, the Powers, the Dominions, Principalities, Archangels, and Angels.

However, there exist other spiritual beings, of which we know little. Rumors abound of a lowly caste known as the Terrae Angeli. A dim shadow of Heavenly Angelic powers and strengths, Terrae Angeli exist only to serve as guardians to man. Four ranks have they: Sage, Guardian, Mentor, and Tiro.

This we know of Terrae Angeli:
Being earthbound, their powers are limited.
Being earthbound, they mirror man in all ways, even unto free will.
Being earthbound, their appearances and powers align to the Four Elements: Wind & Water, Earth & Fire.
Being earthbound, they can destroy and be destroyed.

Translation from the original Latin:
Professor Julian Fitzwilliam
Oxford
1898

Chapter One

GRIFFIN SANG UNDER HIS BREATH as he walked into the kitchen, sneakers in one hand, and dark hair still wet from an early morning shower. Tossing his shoes to one side under the table, he made a beeline for the coffee machine wheezing away on the counter next to the sink. The earthy aroma of coffee mingled with the scent of rain drifting through the half opened window.

Leaning over the sink, he peered out the window across the backyard to the empty field beyond. Heavy, gray clouds filled the sky and clung to the tops of the Rocky Mountains west of High Springs.

The percolator fell silent. He stared at it for a moment, eyes dancing. Grabbing a clean mug from the dishwasher, he filled it half full, then cupped both hands around it and scrunched up his face in concentration.

The coffee began to boil. Brown froth rose to the surface of the cup, bubbles popping. With a grin, he chugged down the superheated drink in one long swig. He smacked his lips, sucked in a deep breath, and held it. *Almost there,* he thought, face turning red. *And now!*

With a snort, he shot plumes of steam out of his

nostrils.

And then his ears.

"That is so awesome," he laughed. Pouring himself a second mug, he glanced up when his Mentor and fellow Terrae Angelus, walked in. "Morning, Basil."

"Fin," Basil replied, using the old nickname. Rain freckled the tall Mentor's worn sweatshirt. *Oxford University* was emblazoned in letters almost faded beyond recognition. Brushing water drops from his cropped white hair, he tossed the morning newspaper, soggy from the May shower, onto the table.

"Hey, watch this," Griffin said, taking another drink and repeating the steaming trick. He threw in a bobbing motion with his head for effect. "Guess what I am?"

"I have no idea." Basil helped himself to the remainder of the coffee.

"I'm a dragon. Get it? Not a griffin, but a dragon."

"Ah. Well. Of course, you are. How dimwitted of me not to have recognized the distinctive nasal emissions. Whatever was I thinking?" He sat down and gingerly peeled open the front page. "You might want to eat breakfast earlier than later. We're on call all weekend."

"Well, I thought it was funny," Griffin muttered under his breath. He stuck his head in the refrigerator and rummaged about. After a few minutes, he emerged with a slice of cold veggie pizza in one hand and a carton of orange juice in the other. He sank down at the table, already chewing; he paused at Basil's expression.

"What?" he asked around a mouthful.

"Orange juice? With pizza?"

"We're out of beer."

Basil snorted. "As if we ever have alcohol in this house."

At that moment, a shaft of Light blazed through the kitchen. Cramming the rest of the slice into his mouth, Griffin jumped up and listened eagerly to the voice speaking from within the beam. When it faded away, he looked at Basil.

"You know, it sounds like a pretty easy mission," Griffin said, shifting from one foot to another. "Probably only needs one of us."

His Mentor sat back, his blue eyes studying Griffin. "Meaning you, I take it?"

"Well, yeah. I mean it's been two months since I was mortal. Now that I'm back in full guardian angel mode *and* sixteen *and* a senior Tiro, shouldn't I be going on more missions by myself?" *Got to let me fly solo sometime, Basil—you can't protect me all the time.*

"Well, I suppose you should." Basil held up a finger in warning. "And remember, no texting while flying."

Griffin gave a whoop and sprinted out the back door. It slammed closed behind him, rattling the window.

With an amused look, Basil returned to his reading. Under the table, he nudged Griffin's shoes to one side. "Any second now," he murmured, folding back another page.

The door flew open. Griffin rushed in, grabbed his shoes, and yanked them on, cursing under his breath while he fumbled with the laces. Scrambling to his feet, he sprinted back out.

Chapter Two

FLYING IN FULL BORE, GRIFFIN SKIDDED to a stop on the rain-slick asphalt of a parking lot. An office building, clearly being remodeled, caught his eyes. Off to one side of the site, a pickup truck sat next to a construction trailer. He looked around and frowned. *So, where's the gig?*

BOOM!

The glass doors of the building blew outward. A split second later, hot wind slapped him in the face. He sprinted toward the structure, trying to ignore the familiar skin-tightening, gut-loosening feeling he got every time he went on a mission. By the time he reached the front, the smoke was billowing out. Crunching through shards, he ran inside.

Flames engulfed the room, some already climbing the walls. Even as Griffin watched, the blaze spread across the bare two-by-fours of the ceiling with a roar.

He glanced upward at the growing inferno and made a face. "Not impressed," he muttered. Squinting through the smoke-filled room, he spied a figure crumpled in the corner, moving feebly. A mangled welding torch lay nearby. He ran over.

"Easy, sir," he said to the man trying to rise. "Let me help you."

Wheezing something about defective tools and incompetent employees, the man coughed as he reached for Griffin's hand. Hauling the worker upright, the angel draped the man's arm over his shoulder and began guiding him toward the door. The flames grew, crinkling hair and crisping clothing. Crying out, the man flung his free arm across his face, shielding it from the intense heat. Griffin slowed to readjust his hold on the man.

A low moan sounded from overhead.

The hairs on the back of Griffin's neck stood at attention. "Oh, crap," he breathed.

Griffin yanked the man back. With a groan, an entire section of the ceiling sagged, then collapsed. Burning timbers, most still attach by only a nail or two, dangled down between them and safety, a blazing barrier. They swayed back and forth, as if daring the pair to try for it.

Blinking sweat from his eyes, Griffin glanced over a shoulder. *Got to find another way out.* He grimaced at the sight of the outer walls, half hidden in the smoke. *If Basil was here, he'd blast a hole right through those cinder blocks with his Might. Well, Basil's not here. And if I ever want to go on another solo mission, I better get this guy out of*—His eyes widened. *Hmmm...blast a hole. It just might work.*

"Sir, I've need you to keep your face covered, okay?" Griffin shouted over the roar of the firestorm. "I've got an idea." *Plus, he doesn't need to see me doing this. After*

13

making sure the worker's eyes were covered, the Terrae Angelus lifted his free arm, tensed his muscles, and pointed at the blazing screen.

Fire erupted from his finger tips. Clenching his jaw, he increased the flow, turning his entire hand into an angelic blowtorch. The force of his Element slammed into the timbers and blew them apart. Burning shrapnel flew everywhere.

"Come on!" Griffin grabbed the man and ran for the door. Side by side, they barreled through the opening, one step ahead of a wall of flames nipping at their heels.

Unable to speak, the man coughed violently as Griffin guided him over to the trailer. He lowered him down onto the folding steps, made sure the man was breathing okay, then pulled out his cell phone.

"Really? Only two bars?" Grumbling under his breath, Griffin stepped around the end of the trailer, eyes intent on the screen. "Finally!" He pressed the speed dial button for the fire department. After relaying the location of the blaze, he hung up.

A *whooshing* sound was the only warning.

Griffin turned around. A chunk of wood filled his vision. Before he could move, the blow snapped his head back. Pain followed a split second later in a white-hot flash. He fell to his knees. Clutching his head, he slumped forward; blood began trickling down his face and along the bridge of his nose from a cut on his left temple. Panting and faintly nauseous, he pushed himself upright after a few minutes. "Oh, Fire," he breathed.

"That hurt."

Swiping at the blood, he staggered to his feet. He kept one hand on the trailer, blinking against the dizziness as he edged around to check on the man. *Good, he's still upright.* In spite of his injury, Griffin grinned weakly. *And cussing out his workers, from the sound of it.* Sighing in relief at the growing wail of the siren, he slipped back behind the trailer. *Time for me to leave.*

With a final glance around, he headed toward the far corner of the parking lot, careful to keep the trailer between himself and the approaching vehicles, and broke into a shambling jog. He picked up speed. With a grunt, he leaped into the air and vanished.

A few minutes later, Griffin landed on hands and knees in his backyard. Sinking to his side, he lay curled on the damp grass, eyes watered from needles of pain stabbing his head in rhythm with his pounding pulse. *I better get inside and clean up before Basil spots me, or I won't see another mission until I'm forty.* He started to sit up when the back door burst open. A tall figure hurried toward him.

"What the bloody hell happened to you?" Basil said with concern. He dropped to one knee.

"Flying debris." Griffin tried to rise. The Mentor's hand on his chest stopped him. He hissed when Basil probed the gash. "But, hey, the mission was a success."

"I should hope so." Basil stood and pulled Griffin up. Keeping a firm grip, he led him toward the house and into the kitchen. "Sit," he ordered, pointing to a chair.

Grabbing the well-used first aid kit from the cabinet, Basil sat down and began cleaning the wound. "It appears you avoided stitches yet again." He applied a butterfly bandage. "But you'll have a black eye for a few days."

Griffin made a face. "Just great. Katie is going to flip out when she sees me tonight." At Basil's confused expression, he added, "Cas Navarre's cousin's Quinceañera? This evening? Remember?"

"Ah, yes." Basil gathered up the medical supplies and began putting them back in the box. "Well, your eye should be a lovely shade of blue-green by this evening, which will go well with your navy blazer." Pushing the kit to one side, he leaned back, face serious. "Care to tell me the details?"

After Griffin finished explaining, he added, "But I have no idea where that chunk of wood came from. It was like someone had..." His voice trailed off.

"Had what?"

"Like...like someone had *thrown* it at me. Sounds weird, I know."

"It does, indeed." He peered closely at Griffin. "How are you feeling now? Any symptoms of a concussion?"

"Nah. You know us Terrae Angeli—we heal in half the time." Griffin grinned at the old saying.

"Thank heaven for that." Basil gestured toward Griffin's blood-splattered tee shirt. "You might want to change, however. That one is a lost cause."

At that moment, the iron knocker on the front door

rapped twice. Before they could move, a woman's voice echoed from the entryway.

"Hello! Anybody home?"

"In the kitchen, Lena," Basil called. He stood up to greet his longtime friend.

Lena Weiss appeared, a brimmed rain hat protecting her gray curls. The aroma of sweet baked apples and cinnamon rose from the foil-covered platter in her hands.

"*Mein Gott*, what has happened to you, *liebling*?" Lena exclaimed, taking in Griffin's battered appearance. "Not a failed mission?"

"Not ducking in time is more like it." He peered hopefully at the plate. "Apple strudel, by any chance?"

"Apple turnovers." Her wrinkled face beamed at the groan of pleasure. She joined him at the table and chuckled when he peeled the foil off and snatched the nearest one. Stuffing half in his mouth, he closed his eyes in contentment.

As Griffin worked his way through the pile, Basil asked Lena, "And how do you like your new place?"

"Oh, it's so much easier to care for than that enormous house. Although I am still sorting through boxes."

"Well, I'm sure Griffin would be happy to help you with..." His voice trailed off as he looked over in disbelief

"What?" Griffin stuffed another pastry into his mouth. A growing pile of flaky crumbs formed a drift in front of him.

"Would you at least *pretend* that I've taught you *some* table manners over the last three years of your apprenticeship?"

Lena laughed at their familiar banter. Rising, she hesitated, holding onto the table. Basil stepped quickly to her side.

"Are you all right?"

"*Ach*, I am fine. Simply too much unpacking." She waved aside Basil's concern. "My new garden is calling for me now that the rain has let up. Griffin, give my love to Katie, yes?"

"I will," he said, sucking a glob of apple filling off a thumb. "And *danke schön* for the turnovers."

"Yes, many thanks," Basil added, glancing mournfully down at the now empty platter. He sighed. "I'm sure they were delicious."

Chapter Three

"BASIL," GRIFFIN HOLLERED AS HE STOOD in front of the bathroom mirror. "I can't get this stupid tie right. It keeps coming out too long on one side." He leaned forward to examine his puffy eye and the cut on his forehead. *I don't care how much faster than humans we heal*, he thought, *it still looks like I went ten rounds*. He scowled at the reflection dressed in a crisp white shirt and dark dress slacks. Yanking the knot loose, he yelled again. "Basil! Frustrated teen here! One who is capable of torching this dumb thing!"

"I would appreciate it, Tiro," Basil said, appearing behind him, "if you would cease bellowing for me." He pushed Griffin's hands away and reached around the apprentice's shoulders. With smooth, precise moves, he finished knotting the tie.

"Thanks." Griffin adjusted it more comfortably and stepped into his room. Plucking a suit coat off the back of the desk chair, he slipped it on and gave it a tug. "So? How do I look?"

"Outside of your injuries, fairly presentable. I'm sure Katie will appreciate your efforts. The Navarre family, too."

"I hope so." He grabbed his cell phone off the dresser and pocketed it. "It's on if you need me."

"And does Katie know we're on call this evening?"

"Yeah. She's cool about it." He paused. "By the way, how *did* you keep in touch with your other Tiros before cells?"

Basil thought for a minute. "Well, most of the time, they were within shouting distance, especially if we were on call."

"I wish you and I could communicate with each other like Flight Command does. That would be cool."

"Are you referring to the angelic *bat signal*?"

"Yup." A corner of Griffin's mouth twitched. "You could be Robin."

Basil chuckled at the old joke. "Not bloody likely. And what time will the Quinceañera be over?"

"I'm not sure, but Katie's curfew is eleven-thirty, so I'll be home right after that."

Griffin headed out of the room, Basil on his heels. After a quick goodbye, he strolled across the street. Reaching Katie's front door, he gave his blazer another tug, then rang the bell.

A deep bark reverberated from inside the house, followed by the scrap of a massive paw rattling the door. He tensed. *Oh, crap*, he thought and took a step back.

"Bear, get away from the door," Katie ordered from inside. "I'm warning you."

The sound of scuffling followed by another thud

made Griffin shake his head. He leaned forward and spoke through the mail flap set in the middle of the door. "Um, we really need to get going."

"I'm trying," she grunted in exasperation, "but he won't budge."

"Ask your dad to hold him."

"He and Mom already left for some professor-and-spouse event at the College." She groaned. "Great. I'm trapped inside my own house by my dog."

"You mean your horse," Griffin muttered. He chewed on the inside of a cheek as he thought. "Hey, I got an idea. Turn off your porch light. I don't want any neighbors to see this." He trotted back down the walkway and turned around. "Okay, open the door," he called, "and let him out."

"Are you kidding?" She yelled back through the mail flap.

"Trust me. And make sure you've got your keys and purse and stuff."

"All right," she said doubtfully. "I hope you know what you're doing."

"Of course, I do. I'm a professional."

The door swung open. A gray-brown behemoth thundered out with a joyous woof. As the wolfhound drew nearer, Griffin crouched slightly, then leaped straight into the air. Bear hurtled past him, just clipping the heels of his dress shoes. With a thump, Griffin landed on the roof. Below him, the dog skidded to a halt in bewilderment.

"Hey, big guy. I'm up here."

Bear whirled around. He began dancing on his back legs, tail wagging with ecstasy at the sight of the Terrae Angelus.

Katie appeared on the porch. "What do I do now?"

"Let me see if I can lure him back inside, then shut the door behind him." Griffin began inching up the slope of the roof.

Bear dropped to all four and hesitated. Then, with a happy yelp, he tore into the house, almost knocking Katie over in his haste to intercept Griffin in the back yard. As the dog shot past her, she gave a shout of triumph and slammed the door closed.

Griffin vanished. He reappeared a second later in the middle of the walkway. "We have got to come up with a better system than..." His voice faded as he locked eyes with his date.

Katie froze at the expression on Griffin's face. "What's wrong?"

He blinked. "Nothing. You just look... insanely... beautiful."

"Really?" Pleased, she glanced down at her blue dress, the same color as her eyes. The simple, snug bodice and narrow straps emphasized her slender form while the skirt flared from her waist, ending just above her knees. She looked up and tucked a pale strand of hair behind one ear. "I was going to wear my hair up in a French twist, but Mom talked me out of it. It would just fall down when we danced anyway." She grinned at Griffin's look of dismay. "And I know how much you love to dance." She peered more closely at his face. "Whoa. Bad mission?"

"Good mission. Bad execution." He took her arm and steered her toward her mom's Bug parked in the driveway. "Come on. We better hurry."

As they walked along, he could feel her eyes on him. He glanced down to make sure everything that should be zipped was zipped and everything that needed to be tucked was tucked. He frowned as she continued to examine him all the way to the car.

"What?"

"You look so different in a suit and tie. Older."

"Really?" He reached around and opened the driver's side door for her. "And just think, I was created only six years ago."

"That still blows my mind." Katie paused, one hand on the car frame. "I mean, why do Terrae Angeli come into existence at ten years old? Why not eight or four or as a baby? Or even as an adult?"

Griffin thought for a moment before answering. "I have no idea. Heck, I never even wondered about it until now. But I guess that's how it is when things are real and not just some made-up fantasy. Reality is uneven and awkward and full of more questions than answers."

"So you don't call this fantasy? That my boyfriend is a guardian angel?"

"Does he have big, white, fluffy wings?"

"Well, no."

"Halo? Harp?"

"No, but..."

"Then it's not fantasy." He helped her in. Careful to not catch her skirt in the door, he closed it, then glanced up. The first stars of the evening blazed like truth in the royal blue of the sky. *And, anyway, reality is way cooler.*

* * *

Pausing in the foyer of the hotel's dining hall, Griffin and Katie looked about, then Griffin let out a low whistle.

"No kidding," Katie breathed.

Below their feet, the dark marble floor twinkled, reflecting the light from an ornate chandelier overhead. The musical clink of silverware on china mingled with the hum of voices drifting through the double doors in front of them. A tuxedoed matrî d smiled politely and held out a gloved hand for their invitation. As Katie pulled it out of her purse, the matrî d did a double take at Griffin.

"I know you," he exclaimed. "You're the young man who dragged me out from under my car. After it had fallen on me in my garage. Last November?"

"I'm sorry, sir." Griffin began, speaking in a well-rehearsed voice. "But, I'm afraid you have mistaken me for someone else." The faintest hint of a British accent colored his words.

The man shook his head. "I was only half conscious, but I distinctly remember your face as you pulled me free. No, it was you." He grabbed Griffin's hand and began shaking it. "Thank you, oh, thank you! I don't know how you managed to get that car off of me!"

"Well, I didn't really—"

"It's because he's an angel."

"Katie," Griffin hissed under his breath.

She ignored him. "Cool, huh?" she said to the man.

"Katie!"

"What? It's true."

"Yeah, but that's my line." His voice bucked up and down from the vigor of the on-going handshaking.

The man faltered with a look of bewilderment. Griffin took the opportunity to ease free. He gestured toward the dining room.

"Um, I think we should probably join the party."

"Oh, yeah. Sorry." The man tugged his tuxedo straight and resumed a formal posture. "Have a lovely evening," he said, eyes still staring. He bowed them inside.

Round tables filled the large area like white, cloth-covered islands. To one side, a buffet stretched the length of the room. Platters and chafing dishes held foods for every taste and desire. At the head table sat a teen girl. Dressed in white and wearing a tiara, she presided as if a princess, surrounded with people all competing for her attention. Her face glowed. She waved cheerfully at Katie and Griffin when they appeared.

"Wow. They really went all out for Michelle's Quinceañera." Katie sighed wistfully. "I wish I could have had a party like this when I turned fifteen. She looks fabulous in that dress, don't you think?"

"Yeah, nice." He craned his neck as he scanned the room. "Do you see Cas anywhere?"

She rolled her eyes, then pointed across the room toward a lanky, black-haired teen. "Over by the buffet."

Winding their way around crowded tables, they dodged waiters and out-of-control children. Griffin fended off several of the younger ones who insisted on wrapping their arms around his knee with delight as soon as they spotted him. Katie laughed when a little boy handed him a soggy cookie. A thread of drool dangled from it.

"Uh, thanks," he said, holding it away from his suit. He patted the child on the head with his free hand. "Just what I always wanted. A half-mouthed gingersnap."

"More cookie." The child scampered away in search of another treat for the angel.

Griffin grimaced. As a waiter scurried past with a full tray of used dishes, he dropped the cookie onto a dirty plate.

"Occupational hazard," Katie pointed out.

"No doubt."

"Hey, Griffin. Katie. Over here." Cas waved at them from the end of the long table, a full plate balanced in one hand. His smile flashed white against his cinnamon skin. "Nice black eye, Raine," he remarked as they joined him. "Katie, you've got to stop beating up on him."

"Nah, he deserved it—maybe next time, he won't be

26

five minutes late." She grinned and reached for an empty plate next to the dessert spread. "Oooh, I'm getting pie first."

"As you should." Griffin stepped into line behind her. He glanced up and down the table, trying to decide between a crab cake and a filet of smoked salmon. With a shrug, he scooped up one of each, then started to reach for a puffy sopapilla.

The familiar tune of *Ring of Fire* trilled from his pocket. He groaned. *Just great—I didn't even get to eat dinner.* Putting the plate down, he tore off a piece of crab cake and popped it in his mouth. He chewed while he pulled out the phone and read the message.

Katie glanced over. Her face fell. "Really?"

"Um...Katie?"

"You've *got* to kidding me," she whispered.

"You know Basil wouldn't have called if he didn't need me," he whispered back.

"But, we just got here."

"I know. And I'm sorry."

She pulled away when he tried to put an arm around her. "And what am I supposed to do? Sit in a corner by myself?" Her voice rose.

"Cas will take care of you."

"I'll take care of what?" Cas looked from Katie to Griffin. "What's up?"

"My dad just texted me." Griffin slipped the phone back into his pocket. "I've got to go. He...he needs help with something that can't wait." He looked at Katie and winced at her growing frustration.

Cas noticed it, too. "Katie, hang with me?"

Before Griffin could speak, she turned and continued filling her plate. "Thanks, Cas—I think I will." She pressed her lips into a thin line. Eyes snapping, she plucked a roll from a basket and threw it on her plate.

Both boys eased back a step.

"Okay, then," Cas said slowly. "I'll just, um, go snag us a table." He hurried off.

An awkward silence fell. Griffin loosed the suddenly too-tight tie and cleared his throat.

"Uh, I better go."

"See you." Without looking back, she stalked away through the crowd toward Cas. As she reached the table, Cas stood up and pulled out a chair for her.

Griffin stood there watching. An odd feeling swept over him—it felt like the emptiness of being hungry, but not quite.

After a moment, he turned on his heels and left.

Chapter Four

STILL HALF HURT, HALF IRRITATED at Katie's reaction, Griffin landed in the backyard a few minutes later. The ground split open with a moan under his feet from the force of the landing. *Sometimes, being a guardian angel sucks.*

Scowling, he stormed across the lawn toward the house, ripping at his tie. With a yank, he pulled it off as he opened the door. "Basil, this had better be the freaking *apocalypse* starting up!" He kicked the door shut behind him. Shame tapped him on the shoulder. *No need to take it out on Basil. It's not his fault.* He ignored it.

After pulling off the suit coat, he tossed it on a kitchen chair and hurried through the house. "Do I have time to change?" he shouted, heading toward the stairs. As his foot touched the first step, Basil spoke behind him from the door of the study.

"Griffin."

"I know, I know. I'm hurrying."

"Griffin. Please."

He froze. Something in his Mentor's voice shot a bolt of alarm through him. He turned around.

The grief etched across Basil's face punched the air out of Griffin's lungs. Gripping the newel post with both hands, he whispered through stiff lips. "What's wrong?"

Stepping closer, the Mentor laid a hand over Griffin's fingers digging into the wood. He cleared his throat. "Lena suffered a sudden massive heart attack an hour ago."

"Is she at the hospital? Is she going to be all right?"

Basil's hand tightened painfully around his for a moment. "No, lad. She...she passed away."

Griffin's legs gave out. With a gasp, he sank down on the step. Basil joined him.

"Are you sure," he asked, struggling to breath. "M-maybe the doctors made a mistake. At the hospital?"

"I wish it were so, but, no."

Staring blankly in front of him, Griffin found himself leaning against his Mentor's shoulder. Suddenly, he felt thirteen again and sick with nausea from another nightmare. His eyes burned. He blinked furiously and scrubbed the back of a hand across them, ducking his head so Basil wouldn't notice. Lost cause.

"There is no shame in tears."

Griffin nodded.

"For either of us."

He nodded again.

"Lena was a remarkable woman who had also overcome much horror in her life. That is why she was so proud of you, Fin. So we will grieve for our loss because we will miss her. And we will rejoice for having known her."

As Griffin sat there, still fighting tears, a memory surfaced. Of Miss Lena stopping by and teaching him sarcastic remarks in German when he was fourteen and confined to the sofa for a few days with multiple fractures in his arm. The corner of his mouth twitched as he recalled the two of them secretly using the phrases around Basil.

"She always called me *liebling*. I acted like it embarrassed me, but it didn't really. I kind of liked it." He sniffed. "I wish I had told her that." *I wish I had told her a lot of things.*

"Oh, she knew. Trust me. She also knew how much you cherished her. As much as she cherished you, lad." He bent his head closer. "And I know this hurts dreadfully at the moment, but, in time, we will speak of her and remember her with smiles, not with sorrow."

"Promise?" Griffin whispered.

"I promise."

A hot tear roll down Griffin's cheek. It landed on the wooden tread with a faint sizzle. As the next one fell, he buried his face in his hands.

* * *

Griffin stared at the cover of the red hymnal tucked in a holder on the back of the pew before him. His eyes traced the gilded letters in an attempt to ignore the groan of the organ launching into another fugue. *I wish Basil would hurry up and get back here*, he thought, glancing toward the front of the church where the Mentor stood speaking with Lena's sister and her family.

Fingers touched his shoulder. He looked behind him.

Katie sat there, her blue eyes bluer with unshed tears. A moment later, Helen and Lewis Heflin slid in next to her. Before sitting down, Helen leaned over. "We're here if you or Basil need anything," she said in a gentle voice.

Griffin nodded once, unable to speak around the lump in his throat. As the family settled, he faced the altar once more. In front of it, a small bronze urn sat on a lace-covered table. Tall flower arrangements on either side guarded it. The thick perfume from the petals made Griffin feel queasy.

After a quiet word with the Heflins, Basil took a seat next to him. He tilted his head toward Griffin and spoke in an undertone. "Would you like Katie to join us?"

"I-I don't know. I mean, I think I just…" *I don't know what I want,* he thought. To his relief, his Mentor simply nodded.

A low murmur, scarcely heard over the organ, filled the church as people spoke softly to another, waiting for the service to begin. Trying to think about something else other than the reason he was there, Griffin glanced over at the mourners across the aisle in the neighboring pew.

One of them caught his attention; a petite, dark-haired woman tastefully dressed in a gray suit. Noticing Griffin, she inclined her head in greeting, her eyes black and almond-shaped, then she lifted a hand from her lap and made a slight motion. To Griffin's surprise, flames flickered on the tips of her fingers before disappearing with another gesture. A tendril of smoke drifted upward. She blew it away before focusing her attention toward the front of the church.

"That's Mentor Nan-ja," Basil said, looking over Griffin's head. "She and her Tiro were re-assigned to High Springs from Denver just recently."

They looked up when the organ stopped. The minister rose from his chair behind the pulpit and walked over to the small table. As he bowed his head in silent prayer, the congregation followed suit.

For several minutes, the only sound was muted weeping and the occasional rustle as people dug for handkerchiefs. *I bet Basil is packing one,* Griffin thought. *All folded perfectly. Probably monogrammed, too.* A bizarre desire to laugh pulled at him. He glanced up, tempted to share the joke.

The Mentor's face was lifted toward the stained glass window decorating the end of the nave. His rugged face was frozen, as if carved from marble. Only his eyes betrayed his sadness. Feeling embarrassed, as if listening uninvited to a private conversation, Griffin looked away.

At that moment, the minister ended his silent prayer with a soft amen and stepped closer to the urn. The congregation stilled when he began the eulogy.

Half-listening to the words, Griffin's thoughts drifted like the smoke from Mentor Nan-ja's Fire. He felt alone in his grief. *I wonder if she knows we're all here right now thinking about her. I wonder if she misses us. Like we miss her?*

Basil's Journal: Monday, May 23rd

These last few days have been numbing. Today's memorial service was heartbreaking for both of us. Ah, Lena, it was an honor to have called you friend.

"...flights of angels sing thee to thy rest."

Griffin's Journal: Monday, May 23rd

I've never had a family. At least, not in the way humans define family. But I think I know what it's like to have a father.

And an aunt.

Auf Wiedersehen, meine tante.

Chapter Five

WITH A SIGH, GRIFFIN PUSHED AWAY from his desk. Crawling back into bed, he curled on one side and pulled the quilt over his head, trying to block out the glow from the streetlamp outside the window. A heaviness pressed him down against the mattress.

The floorboards creaked. A soft knock on his door followed a moment later. He pulled the covers tighter when it opened.

"Fin?" Basil called softly. "Are you awake, lad?"

"I really don't feel like talking," he said through the quilt. He held his breath, then let it out at the sound of the door closing with a faint click.

An hour later, he gave up on sleep. Kicking the quilt to one side, he rolled out of bed and pulled on a tee shirt and sweatpants, then made his way downstairs to the kitchen. Noticing the back door ajar, he headed outside.

Basil stood in the center of the yard, facing westward, a black shape in the pre-dawn light. Lifting his face to the sky, he stretched out his arms and rotated his hands in a circular motion. Leaves and twigs and bits of dried grass began to swirl around his bare feet in an eddy of Wind. He gestured again. With a soft sigh, the Wind increased. Debris whirled around him even faster, rising higher and higher until he stood in the very center of a vortex.

After a long minute, Water gushed from his fingertips in powerful streams. It mingled with the Wind. They began twisting around each other in a double helix of Elements.

At a final gesture from the Terrae Angelus, the geyser soared upward, elongating as it went. It climbed like an arrow, higher and higher until it faded from sight amongst the morning stars.

"Whoa." Griffin watched, spellbound, until it disappeared. "What was that?"

Basil glanced over a shoulder. "Oh, a bit of a homage." He dried wet fingers on his jeans. "And how are you feeling?"

"Like I want to sleep, but I can't." Griffin walked over and joined the Mentor. "I wish we could go on a mission, so I could think about something else."

"Then why don't I inform Flight Command to put us back on rotation tonight. If you are certain you're ready."

"I am." Looking down, he dug his toes into the cool lawn and sighed. "It all seems so weird."

"Weird in what way?"

"It's just hard to believe that I'll never talk with Miss Lena again."

"I feel the loss as well." They stood together in silence watching as the dawn colored the city and mountains beyond in shades of lavenders and pinks.

"Basil?"

"Fin."

"What happens to us when we die?"

"Well, after a few hours, our bodies return to the Elements from which we came. 'Ashes to ashes, dust to dust,' as they say. Our labors finished, and our rest deserved."

"Like falling asleep?"

"Perhaps. Or maybe it will be more like waking up from a dream."

Griffin nodded. He thought for a moment before speaking. "Are you afraid to die?"

The Mentor shook his head. "Heavens, no. Life and death are simply two hands holding us between them. I do not fear life. Therefore, I do not fear death."

As the day brightened around him, Griffin thought about his master's word. *Maybe he's right. Maybe death is just like a new day, stretching out before us.*

* * *

"What's the word?" Griffin looked up from the television when Basil walked into the living room from the study across the hall.

"We are now on call." He plucked the remote from Griffin's hand, then sank down in his favorite wingback chair by the fire crackling in the grate. The sweet aroma of burning pine filled the room. "Beginning at seven this evening." He changed the channel.

"Hey, I was watching the game."

"Now, you are watching the news."

Griffin made a face.

Basil ignored him. "Say, why don't you go visit Katie for a bit? You two haven't spent much time together for these last few days except for those minutes at the memorial service. I'll ring you if you're needed."

As Griffin walked across the street through the cool evening, a memory from last Christmas suddenly swept over him. A memory of Miss Lena spending an evening showing Katie and him how to bake gingerbread men. He grinned when he recalled Katie molding the soft doughy figures into all kind of silly positions. *The man using his own head as a basketball was my favorite.*

"Hello, Griffin." Lewis answered the doorbell, reading glasses perched on top of his bald head and a newspaper in one hand. "How are you doing, son?"

"Okay, I guess. And thank you, and Mrs. Heflin, for coming to the service. It meant a lot to Basil and me."

"Of course. And if there is anything else we can do, let us know." With a tilt of his head, he gestured down the hall. "They're in the den." Before Griffin could ask who *they* were, the professor ambled back to the living room.

Frowning in confusion, Griffin headed toward the rear of the house. He slammed to a stop when Cas' voice floated out of the room, followed by Katie's giggle.

"No, stupid," Cas said. "You're supposed to list the formula for each step in order. Man, you are so going to fail your final."

"Gee, thanks for the vote of confidence," Katie replied over the sound of clacking keys. "Okay, is this right?"

"Scoot your skinny self over and let me see."

"I wouldn't talk about skinny if I were you, Stick-man." Laughter followed.

"Stick-man? Oh, thanks a lot. So what do you call Raine?"

"Angel Boy, of course."

"Like that makes any sense. Is it because he always walks the straight and narrow?"

"Hey, I thought he was your friend."

"He is. He's cool, but come on. You're the one who called him a choir boy at Michelle's party."

Anger, and a sense of betrayal, uncoiled in Griffin's chest like a snake. Eyes flashing with a brown fire, he eased forward on silent feet.

Squeezed together on the single desk chair with their backs to him, Cas and Katie sat working in front of the computer. As she bent over the keyboard, clacking away, Griffin caught a glimpse of his own blurred figure reflected on the screen. Looking up, Katie jumped, then let out a squeak. Before she could turn around, Griffin stepped back from the doorway and vanished.

A moment later, he materialized in Katie's front yard with a thump. Chest heaving from the abrupt flight, he stood there in the darkness, fighting an unexpected mix of rage and embarrassment.

I don't believe it, he thought, storming back across the street. *They're sitting over there talking about me like...like...I'm some kind of goody two-shoe.* "While I'm out here risking my butt to help you mortals," he shouted aloud. Spying a plastic soda bottle in the gutter, he threw out an arm and pointed his hand at it.

A torrent of flames erupted from the tips of his fingers. Fire ignited the bottle and blasted it into the air, the stink of melting plastic souring the evening air. It landed with a hiss in a nearby puddle. He grunted in satisfaction and stomped up the steps of the porch.

*   *   *

Basil winced when the front door opened, then shut with a crash, rattling the windows. He looked up as Griffin marched past the archway.

"I take it something is amiss?" He blinked in surprise when Griffin continued upstairs, trailing a string of muted cuss words. The slamming of the bedroom door followed a moment later.

By the Light, I would not have guessed he even knew those words, Basil thought. *On the other hand, he did spend several weeks in a public high school.* He stood up with a sigh as he mentally steeled himself for the upcoming clash. *Nonetheless, that is not acceptable behavior*

A beam of Light illuminated the living room. Basil groaned. "Oh, brilliant timing." He listened while the voice within the beam spoke, then lifted his head toward the ceiling. "Griffin," he called. "We've been summoned." As the sound of pounding feet echoed from overhead, he stepped into the entryway and wait, one hand on the door handle. An eyebrow shot up when Griffin appeared, still glowering and body stiff with anger.

Basil tightened his jaw and locked eyes with the apprentice. Griffin raised his chin and glared back.

"What?"

"What do you think, Tiro?"

"Not a clue. *Mentor.*"

"Hazard a guess."

"Why don't you just tell me already?" Griffin's voice rose in frustration. "So we can stop screwing around and get on with the mission."

Without a word, Basil turned and opened the front door. When Griffin started to follow, he pushed the apprentice back inside.

"No, you are not coming. I'll not have a Tiro along on such a volatile mission when his focus is clearly on personal issues. Not when a mortal's life is at stake."

Shutting the door on Griffin's astonished face, he stepped to the edge of the porch and vanished into the night.

* * *

The two young men stood nose to nose, breathing beer fumes into each other's faces and surrounded by a growing crowd. The neon light from the bar's green parrot sign illuminated part of the alley. As the mob began chanting *fight, fight,* the first one cocked a fist back.

A tall figure stepped out of the mass of onlookers and pushed between the men. He grabbed the first man's wrist in an iron grip.

"Steady on. No need to resort to violence." Basil forced them further apart. "Say, how about a few rounds of rock-paper-scissors to settle your dispute, eh?"

The crowd laughed at the suggestion, Taking advantage of the distraction, the second man lunged around Basil for his opponent.

Basil threw out his free hand, palm forward. The man's feet left the pavement from the force of the Terrae Angelus' Might. He flew backward, over the heads of the onlookers, and slammed onto the adjacent building. With a dull thud, he hit the brick wall, then folded into a boneless heap.

At that moment, the first man jerked loose of Basil's hold. Scrambling away, he pulled out a switchblade. *Click.* It sprang open.

"How *West Side Story*," Basil murmured.

The sight of the knife sent the crowd scattering. Most ran from the scene while a few hurried back around the corner into the bar for a final beer before the police arrived.

As the man danced around him, jeering at him to *bring it, old man*, Basil shook his head. "I would put that weapon away before you injure yourself."

"Not *me*, dude. *You*. I'm gonna cut you." He tossed the knife from hand to hand.

"Highly doubtful. But I applaud your enthusiasm, nonetheless. One should always have goals." Basil started toward the man. "But enough of this. Now, why don't you hand me your weapon and we'll—"

A force clipped the back of his knees, sending Basil off balance. He stumbled, almost hitting the side of the building. Catching himself with both hands, he whirled around to confront the new threat.

At that moment, the man darted forward, and slashed the knife across Basil's ribs.

Chapter Six

Back At The House, Griffin Stared at the door. "I don't believe it." For a minute, he hesitated. Then, with a snarl, he yanked it open and shot outside. *No way. You're not going without me to watch your back.* In a blast of hot wind, he vaulted one-handed over the porch railing and vanished.

Materializing at the far end of the alley, he staggered a step when he landed on something moist and slippery. *Ewww. I don't want to know.* Hearing Basil's voice, he ducked behind a dumpster and crouched down. A foul stench wafted from the bin. He wrinkled his nose and tried to breathe through his mouth.

As the Mentor's voice continued to echo along the narrow brick canyon, Griffin relaxed. *Well, I guess he's okay since he's preaching to the guy. I wonder if I should just go back home.* He peeked around the container. At that moment, the man stabbed his Mentor.

"Basil!" Griffin leaped up and sprinted toward them. Terror filled his mouth with a foul taste. *We're not totally impervious to injuries, or even death, lad.* A memory from his earliest days as an apprentice whispered in his head.

In spite of our abilities, too many Terrae Angeli die in the field.

The assailant whirled around at the shout, then ran out of the alley. Griffin ignored him. He skidded to a halt beside the Mentor sagging against the wall, a hand pressed to his side.

"Oh, Fire," Griffin choked. "How bad is it?"

"What the blazes are you doing here?" Basil hissed when Griffin pulled the hand away to examine the wound. "Leave it for now. We'll take care of this at home." He glanced around the alley. "In more sterile conditions, eh?"

"Can you fly?"

"I believe so." He straightened up with a grimace. He kept a hand on Griffin's shoulder for support.

"Or I could try to carry you," added Griffin doubtfully. "But my record on hauling anything during flight is still hit-or-miss."

"No need to endanger me further." He took a deep breath. "A moment, please." Reaching into a back pocket with his free hand, he pulled out a handkerchief and pressed it against the wound.

Griffin looked around. "We're clear for take-off if you're ready."

Basil nodded and tightened his grip. "Right."

Side by side, they began walking toward the back of the alley. They broke into a jog. As they reached the end, they both leaped into the air and vanished.

Reappearing on the front porch a few minutes later, Griffin seized Basil's arm when the Mentor abruptly sagged. Opening the door, he pulled him across the threshold and lowered him down onto the hallway bench. Blood stained the entire side of Basil's white shirt. "Hey—you still with me?"

Basil raised his bowed head. "I am. But it does hurt like the very dickens," he said through pale lips. "And I'm afraid this shirt may be ruined."

"You were lucky the guy was too drunk to do more than gouge you a good one."

"Fetch the kit, eh?" When Griffin hesitated, he waved a hand in dismissal. "I'll be fine. It just requires a few sutures."

"Well, well," boomed a voice. "Looks like I came at the right time." They looked up in surprise.

Sukalli stood in the doorway in his signature fringed leather jacket. His enormous bulk filled the space. Stepping inside, his black eyes narrowed at the sight of Basil slumped on the bench. "What happened?"

As Griffin explained, the Guardian squatted down on the heels of his cowboy boots in front of Basil. A hawk feather dangled from the leather tie holding back his long black ponytail. He pulled up the Mentor's shirt and poked at the wound. "Don't be such a girl," he joked when Basil winced. He stabbed a thumb over a shoulder. "Be a good time for this young one to practice his sewing."

Griffin blanched. "I...I can't."

"Sure you can." The Guardian nodded toward the

kitchen. "Go get your gear."

At Basil's nod, Griffin hurried to the kitchen and grabbed the well-stocked first aid kit. When he returned, Sukalli was sitting next to his friend.

"Looks like your Mentor will only need five or six stitches." He flipped open the box and began rummaging through it. Whistling softly between his teeth, he pulled out several items.

Griffin gazed wide-eyed as Sukalli began threading a curved needle. He swallowed. "Uh, couldn't I just watch you do it this time?" He edged backwards.

"No time like the present to practice." He paused, the needle in one hand and an antiseptic wipe in the other. "You want to do this here or in the bathroom?"

"Neither." Griffin took another step back.

"Look, pup, learning basic first aid is part of being an apprentice. So suck it up and get over here." He changed tactics when Griffin refused to move. "Or are you going to wimp out on your Mentor?"

"Is wimping out an option?" he asked, eyes glued to the needle.

"By the Light," Basil growled, snatching the wipe from Sukalli. He ran it across his ribs, wincing at the sting, and held it there to absorb the seeping blood. One-handed, he grabbed a bandage from the kit, ripped the paper wrapping off with his teeth, and applied it to the top section of the wound. "There. Now, Griffin, I'll need three more just like that." He handed the rest of the butterfly bandages over and lifted his arm out of the way. "I would have bled to death by the time you two finished."

As Griffin began bandaging the Mentor, Sukalli stood up and moved to one side. "How did you get the shiner?" he asked, studying the apprentice's faded bruise.

"Got hurt on a mission." Finished, Griffin threw the rest of the bandages into the box. He replaced the needle in its tiny case with a shudder and closed the lid. "Anything else I should do?"

"I could use a bit of healing Might." Basil rolled his eyes when Griffin began protesting.

"Oh, come on, Basil! I suck at Might use."

"All the more reason to practice."

"Fine," he grumbled. "But when nothing happens and you get gangrene or something, I want it officially noted that I did this under protest."

The corner of Basil's mouth twitched. "So noted."

Sitting down next to him, Griffin laid a hand against his Mentor's side. He closed his eyes and took a deep breath, brows knitted together in concentration.

"You're trying too hard, Fin. Calm down and focus within. Think of yourself as a vessel, being filled with Might. Once filled, let its power flow through you to wherever or however it is needed."

"Sounds like a toilet," he said under his breath.

"I heard that."

Griffin grinned. He willed himself to relax. A bubble of *something* he could never quite describe welled up inside of him. It spread through his body in a warm flood, reaching to the tips of his fingers. His palm began to tingle where it pressed against the wound. He opened his eyes in triumph.

Then the tingling stopped.

He dropped his hand in defeat. "See? I told you. I can't do it."

"Actually, you did," Basil pointed out. "You just couldn't *maintain* it. Remember, Might use is a highly advanced skill—yours will come in time."

"Want some help, brother?" Sukalli asked.

"Thank you, but no. I'll tend to it later." He tugged the torn and bloody shirt back into place. "I assume this is not a social call."

"M'afraid not. Let's talk in the living room." Sukalli slid a hand under Basil's elbow and helped him up.

They made their way through the archway. The Guardian took a seat on the sofa while Basil chose the wingback by the fireplace. Nearby, Griffin perched on the arm of another chair. Sukalli sat in silence, a grave expression on his bronze face.

"Well?" prompted Basil.

"I've just come from a meeting with Flight Command," Sukalli began. "Our old friend was there."

"Nicopolis?" Basil's face hardened. He and Griffin exchanged glances.

"Yup."

"Curious. I wasn't aware that he was back from the Middle East."

"He's been back for a week or so."

49

"And may I inquiry as to the nature of the meeting?"

"Well, it's official," Sukalli said. "Command has stripped Nicopolis of his rank."

"Yes!" Griffin punched a fist into the air.

"How did he take it?" Basil asked.

"How do you think? He howled like a coyote about the unfairness of it all, accused you both, especially Griffin, of ruining him. Then he swore he was done with the Terrae Angeli once and for all."

"Hey, can we get that in writing?" Griffin's grin faded when his Mentor glared at him.

"Hardly a laughing matter, Tiro. Nicopolis is more dangerous to us now than ever before."

"Why?"

"Because Flight Command kept him reined in," Sukalli explained. "Now he is free of any hobbles."

"How can he do that? Stop being a Terrae Angeli?"

"Because, like the mortals we serve, we have free will," Basil explained. "We have the right to choose the directions of our lives. For good or for bad."

"And Nicopolis has picked a bad trail to follow. In fact, I wouldn't put it past him to make an attempt at the pup here when your guard is down, old friend."

Griffin frowned. "An attempt at what?"

The Terrae Angeli looked at each other for a long minute before Basil answered. "Revenge. And possibly, murder, lad."

Icy fingers stroked the back of Griffin's neck. He swallowed. "So what do we do?"

"Well, to start with, take what I told you with a grain of salt. Nicopolis knows he's no match for Basil in a straight up fight. He's probably just crying at the moon. But until I can figure out what he's up to, no more solo missions for you. Either of you." Sukalli ignored Griffin's squawk of protest and continued. "I want both of you watching each other's backs. You lay low and let those wounds heal before Nicopolis tries to add new ones."

Griffin groaned. "For how long?"

"Depends on how long you want to live."

Chapter Seven

AT THAT MOMENT, THE METALLIC RATTLE and clank of the door's iron knocker sounded. Basil gave a nod of permission. Griffin stepped into the entryway and opened the door.

Katie stood there, arms wrapped around her middle. "We need to talk," she said in a quiet voice.

"About what?"

"About earlier. About you overhearing me and Cas." She shifted from foot to foot.

He opened his mouth, then froze as he glanced past her shoulder. Heat swelled his chest at the sight of Cas' car parked in front of her house. "What's he still doing there?"

"We're studying for our science final."

"Sure you are."

Her cheeks flushed. "Listen, I wanted to apologize for what I said. I guess I was still mad about the party."

"Yeah, well. Sorry my *choir boy* stuff puts a crimp in your social life. But hey, I like the way you had a second guy already lined up." He started to close the door.

She slapped her hand against it and gave it a shove.

"You know, you might want to try looking at all this from *my* point of view." Her voice rose in frustration. "It's kind of hard having a boyfriend who puts everyone else before me."

"It's who I am," he yelled. "I'm a guardian angel."

"Well, sometimes I wish you weren't," she shouted back.

The words poisoned the air between them.

With a growl of frustration, Katie spun on her heels and stomped away. Griffin watched in silence. With a sick heart, he shut the door and leaned back against it.

Oh, please don't mean that.

After a moment, he closed his eyes and began dribbling his head on the oak panel. The pain felt good.

"Griffin?"

He stopped and opened his eyes. Sukalli stood in the archway.

"I guess you heard us."

"Hard to miss when you two were yowling at each other like a pair of polecats." He gestured toward the living room. "Now get your tail in here and reassure your mommy of a Mentor that you're okay."

In spite of the residual anger inside, Griffin smiled weakly and followed the Guardian. "I'm good," he said to Basil as he walked past and resumed his seat. "Katie and I just..." His voice trailed off.

"No need to explain." Much to Griffin's relief, Basil dropped the subject and turned back toward Sukalli. He studied his old friend's face. "There's something else, isn't there?"

"Just something Nicopolis said that's been boring into my skull like a sand tick. In a melodramatic performance, he had hollered that the Terrae Angeli will be sorry. That he found something that will make him more powerful than even the Sages."

"Let me guess—a magic ring?" Griffin said.

Basil and Sukalli looked at each other in confusion.

At that moment, a beam of Light illuminated the room. A quiet voice spoke from within. When Basil began to push himself upright, Sukalli shook his head.

"Hold your horses, brother. You're not going any-where—not until you've healed up a bit. And don't make me pull rank on you," he added when the Mentor protested.

"The only reason you outrank me is because I refused promotion," Basil said, sinking back down. "Of course, it was the best decision I ever made."

"You had a chance to be a Guardian and you turned it down?" Griffin said in disbelief. "Why?"

Before Basil could speak, Sukalli interrupted him. "You two sit this one out—I'll take this call." Without an-other word, he took a step and disappeared in a soft puff.

Basil's Journal: Tuesday, May 24th

Nicopolis. We cannot seem to shake free of that viper. And it is not like Sukalli to be so cautious. He suspects something. What it is, I am not sure.

Griffin's Journal: Tuesday, May 24th

Fire, could anything else go wrong in my life? First,

Miss Lena. Then Basil gets hurt. Then Nicopolis goes psycho AGAIN and maybe wants to kill us AGAIN, so we get banned from solo missions by Guardian Sukalli.

And I want to see Katie so bad right now. Just to try to make everything okay. But does she want to see me?

Katie's Journal: Tuesday, May 24th

I don't like feeling this way. I was mad at him earlier, but now I'm scared. Scared that we are growing apart. I want things to be the way they were when he was a mortal. I want things to go back to the way they were… before.

But he was so sad then.

Does this mean for me to be happy, he has to be miserable?

* * *

Closing her laptop, Katie stood up and turned off her desk lamp. Winding her way through the darkened room around islands of clothes, she threw herself on her messy bed, not bothering to close the blinds. "I hate my life," she complained to the ceiling.

She squeaked when a figure appeared outside her window. Landing in front of the dormer, it blocked out the stars.

"Crap, that scares me every time he does that," she muttered. Rolling off her bed, she stumbled across her messy floor. She signaled Griffin to step back, then cranked open the casement.

"Hey."

55

"Hey." Griffin squatted down on the sloping roof. Dark tee shirt and jeans made him almost invisible in the night.

For a long minute, they struggled to look at each other through the open window. Then, Griffin took her hand resting on the sill. His fingers, always a few degrees warmer than humans, squeezed hers. "Sorry."

"Yeah, me, too. I really didn't mean it when I said... what I said."

Griffin smiled. "Sure you did."

Katie's jaw dropped.

"Look, I get it. I really do," Griffin said. "And I'm not saying this to make you feel guilty or anything, but you have to admit, it would be a lot easier on you if I was just a regular human guy, right?"

Katie nodded, unable to breathe from fear of his next words.

"But I'm not. And I never will be. I don't *want* to be."

"I know."

"So...so, do you want to go out with Cas?" Griffin blurted out. "Instead of me?"

"No! Griffin, he just came over to study for finals. That's all. We're friends. Nothing more. Okay?"

Griffin let out a long breath. "We're going to have to work like crazy to keep this going between us." He looked away. "I mean, if you still want to."

Katie blinked as tears prickled her eyelids. "More than anything," she whispered.

"Good." He glanced back over a shoulder. "Look, I've got to get back. Basil got hurt earlier—"

"Oh, my gosh—is he okay?"

"Yeah, just a knife wound. But he doesn't know I'm over here and if he needs me, I want to be available." He hesitated, started to say something, then stopped.

"What is it?"

"Um, just so you know. Nicopolis was stripped of his rank as a Mentor by Flight Command—"

"About time."

"—and went ballistic. Sukalli thinks he may be coming after me and Basil." He squeezed her hand again when she gasped. "Hey, it's okay. You know we can handle that nut case."

"Can't Flight Command just send some of those what-do-you-call-them...Sages...after Nicopolis and take away his powers or something?"

"Well, for one thing, there are only a few Sages in the world and they are busy dealing with a lot worse problems than this. And Command *is* trying to find Nicopolis. But in the meantime, we'll just have to keep our eyes open. And stop worrying." He grinned. "We're the good guys, remember?"

Katie's heart skipped a beat at his smile. "All right. But just be careful." She closed her eyes as Griffin leaned forward and wrapped his arms around her for a brief hug. Keeping her eyes closed, she felt a puff of warm air ruffle her hair when he vanished a moment later.

For a long time, she stood in the window, breathing in the lingering scent of Earth and Fire. Until it faded away.

Chapter Eight

THE NEXT AFTERNOON, BASIL STOOD in front of his bathroom mirror, shirt pulled up on one side while he examined the knife wound. With a grunt of satisfaction, he began peeling the bandages off one by one.

Griffin appeared in the doorway. "How is it?"

"Take a look."

He peered closely, then shook his head. "It's practically healed already. Just a scar." He looked up at the Mentor. "Are we back on call?"

"I've already spoken with Sukalli. He agreed to put us in duty rotation after I reassured him that neither of us will attempt solo missions for awhile." Basil smoothed his shirt into place. "But you and I need to talk about these coming days." He motioned Griffin to follow him downstairs.

"Uh-oh, this sounds like it'll take awhile. Let me grab a snack." Griffin disappeared into the kitchen while Basil continued on to the study.

After a minute, his apprentice joined him, a half-eaten brownie in one hand. Flopping down on the sofa, Griffin chewed as he glanced out the wide windows overlooking the porch. Thunder rumbled. The room darkened as clouds built up over the city, a prelude to High Springs' daily afternoon rainstorm.

Basil sat at his desk, chair creaking as he rocked back. His gaze fell upon the scar on the edge of Griffin' lower lip, then on the pastry in the teen's hand.

The memory of their very first hour together, after he had rescued the lad from the abusive Nicopolis, rose in Basil's mind. A memory of watching as a thirteen-year-old Griffin, the most recent blow from his former mentor still raw on his face, had edged into the kitchen.

Basil finished setting a platter of sandwiches and a carton of cranberry juice on the table when he caught a movement by the kitchen doorway. "Ah, there you are, Tiro. I was afraid you might have gotten lost betwixt here and your bedroom. All washed up?"

Griffin nodded, eyes wary.

"Shall we eat, then?" With a wave of his hand, he indicated the seat across from him and sat down.

He peeked out of the corner of his eye as Griffin slid around the table, keeping the maximum distance between himself and the Mentor as possible. The youth perched on the edge of the chair and waited.

"Well, tuck in. You'll find tuna salad in the sandwiches nearest to you." Basil nodded toward the plate. Eyebrows rose when Griffin grabbed the nearest sandwich and fell upon it, almost choking as he wolfed it down. By the Light, when did he eat last? *"Hungry, eh?"*

Griffin nodded again. He kept a tight grip on the rest of

the sandwich as he hammered down on his meal. With the other hand, he pushed overgrown bangs out of his eyes, the dark hair filthy and matted.

"Would you care for juice?"

"Yes, sir." Griffin's voice sounded rusty, unused.

Trying to ignore a growing suspicion, Basil poured juice for both of them. He slid a glass over, covertly studying the Tiro's torn and grimy clothing, fingernails chewed to a pulp. The air of nervousness. His eyes traveled down to the injury on the young face. Griffin froze in mid-chew when he noticed Basil looking at him.

"That cut by your lip, lad? How old is it?"

Griffin swallowed with difficulty. "A few days, Mentor," he said, voice scarcely above a whisper.

"And how did you get it?" I can guess how he came by it, Basil thought. But I'm curious as to his reaction to the question.

Shame flooded Griffin's face. "I-I ran into something."

Basil nodded, not willing to press the issue. For now. "Of course." Rising, he stepped over the counter and picked up a white bakery box. He placed it on the table and flipped the lid open, revealing an assortment of pastries. "Please help yourself. I wasn't sure what you preferred, so I chose a variety. Have you a favorite?"

Griffin shook his head.

"Do you mean you do not have a favorite or you do not care for any?"

"I-I've never eaten anything like those."

"Oh." Basil's heart twisted. He forced a smile. "Well, you

look like a chocolate aficionado to me." He selected a fudgey delight and slipped it on his apprentice's plate.

One hand still grasping the half-eaten sandwich, Griffin picked up the brownie and took a careful bite. He chewed. Then, wonder spread across his face.

"Good, eh?"

"Yes, sir." Griffin took a bigger bite. He finished it off and licked his fingers.

"Have more. Of everything."

For the next ten minutes, Basil watched in astonishment as Griffin polished off two sandwiches, another glass of juice, and four brownies. Followed by a glass of milk.

Still lost in thought, a corner of Basil's mouth twitched when he recalled Griffin falling asleep in the Saab on the way to the store for new clothes later that day, overcome by a full stomach. *Probably for the first time in years, poor lad.*

He blinked and looked around the study when an amused voice spoke.

"Hel-loooow!" Griffin waved a hand back and forth. "Earth to Basil." He grinned. "Literally."

The Mentor forced himself into the present. Clearing his throat, he straightened up. "Where were we?"

"Well, I'm not sure where *you* were just now—"

"Not important."

"—but I'll bet you were about to tell me that I need to be careful. But to keep things in perspective because that wacko may just being blowing smoke. And, probably, you were also going to remind me that between the two of us, we can handle anything that comes our way. Because we always have and we always will." He made a flapping motion with his hands. "You know. Go Team Angel and all that."

Basil laughed. "Oh, well said, Tiro, in spite of the rather odd hand gesture. You certainly touched on the major points I would have covered."

"Yeah, so stop worrying about me. I'm not that screwed up apprentice I was three years ago. This is what I have been training my whole life to handle."

"Speaking of training, I think it is time we step up yours. Both for your own protection and as part of your apprenticeship."

"What kind of—" Griffin stopped when the beam of Light shot between them. They listened intently.

"Right. We're leaving now," Basil said as it faded away. They rose to their feet and headed through the house to the kitchen. Lightning cracked overhead as the rainstorm broke open; a rumble of thunder followed a moment later. Griffin opened the back door.

"Tally ho," he cried in a perfect imitation of his Mentor.

"Cheeky," replied Basil, unable to quell his slight smile.

Together, they vanished into the storm.

* * *

The delivery van raced down the highway. Its tires sprayed water over nearby windshields and blinded the more cautious drivers as they crept through the afternoon's rush hour. Wipers slapped at the increasing rain while drivers hunched over their steering wheels. Up and down the four lanes, headlights began flipping on like fireflies in random patterns.

Hitting a watery patch, the van hydroplaned, losing its grip on the road. Without warning, it slewed sideways into the compact car in the next lane and clipped its front end. Both vehicles spun off the highway.

The car's tires left the ground. It landed with a crash, miraculously still upright, then bounced down the steep embankment. It jolted to a stop ten yards from the roadside.

Meanwhile, the van rolled over and plowed further down the slope on its side, mud churning in its wake. It stopped. Despite the deluge of rain, flames began licking at the engine, fanned by the wind. Smoke swirled through the cab. The driver coughed as he fought to free his trapped legs. Broken glass lay scattered about the inside of the cab, reflecting the flames' red colors like rubies.

"I've got this one," shouted a voice; a pair of feet appeared outside the wreckage. The driver craned his head around. A teenage boy crouched down by the windshield, dark brown hair ruffled by the storm.

"We're going get you out, sir. Just stay calm." Griffin pulled off his jacket and wrapped it around his right hand. Grasping the edge of the shattered windshield, he tore away a part of it away, glass in large flakes. Pieces disintegrated, raining down on the battered driver. "Sorry about that," he said. He braced a foot against the frame and tugged at the next section, the fire roaring louder.

"Kid, get out of here. It's going to blow any minute!" The driver reached down and grasped his pant leg, trying to yank free from the crumbled dashboard.

"Almost got it." Griffin cursed when his jacket-wrapped hand slipped a second time. Sucking in a deep breath, he focused his Might and pulled again. "Come on!" he growled in frustration.

* * *

Up the hill, Basil grasped the handle of the car and yanked the door open. A middle aged woman looked up at him, her eyes wide with shock. "Are you all right?" he asked.

"I-I think so," she said breathlessly. "My wrist hurts a little. I guess I hit it on the steering wheel."

"Here. Give me your other hand." He helped her out of the vehicle, took off his jacket, and wrapped it around her. Glancing back over a shoulder, he narrowed his eyes at the sight of the van and growing flames.

"What can I do?" A young woman rushed over, her jeans already splattered by the mud and a small first aid kit clasped in one hand. Her nearby sedan, its red emergency lights flashing on and off, sat parked on an angle on the shoulder.

"Stay with her, miss. I'll return momentarily." Basil

spun around and bolted down the hill.

* * *

Griffin blinked, sweat and rain running into his eyes. Pausing, he peered over the wreck at the spreading fire. His heart leaped with relief as he spied his Mentor hurrying toward him.

"I can't free him," he gasped when Basil arrived. "His legs are trapped. You better put that out—it's about to reach the tank!"

Basil squatted down and nudged Griffin aside. "You cannot extinguish a gasoline fire with water." He reached through the shattered windshield and grabbed the lip of the dashboard. Metal screeched as he began ripping the crumbled van apart. "Instead, I want you to muster the largest load of dirt you can and smother it."

Griffin raced further down the slope, away from the highway, and disappeared into the darkness. *I doubt anyone is going to notice what I'm doing*, he thought. *Not in this storm.* He fell to his knees and dug the heels of both hands into the mud. With a grunt, he shoved the ground in front of him, muscles straining against the inertia of the Earth, willing it to obey him. "Move already!" He dug his toes into the ground and pushed harder. A pile of sodden dirt, half the size of the van, suddenly let loose and flew through the air. It slopped over the van. A second one followed, then a third, soaring through the air like giant scoops of chocolate ice cream.

Panting from the effort, Griffin dumped load after

load of dripping soil on the engine. Wind-blown mud splattered his face and body. As the flames faltered, he launched a few more, halting when the last of the inferno died down. In the distance, he could hear the scream of the approaching ambulance cutting through the night.

Griffin nodded in satisfaction as he watched Basil slide the man free of the wreckage. After a brief conference, the Mentor straightened, helped the man to his feet, then led him up the slope and away from the vehicle. Reaching the shoulder of the road and the growing crowd, he handed off the man to a helpful Samaritan and turned around.

Grinning through the muck, Griffin walked out of the shadows and paused next to the van. Catching his Mentor's attention, he held up filthy hands. "Hey," he called, voice full of laughter. "Think you could hose some of this off of me?"

At that moment, all hell broke loose.

The van exploded.

A fireball shot upward in a boiling mass of flames. A second later, scorching wind slapped the spectators. Some fell to the ground.

The blast punched Griffin square in the chest and stomach. His feet left the ground. With a grunt, he flew backwards toward the high concrete wall separating the highway from the residential area beyond. Red filled his world when the flames enveloped him in a roar, muting the rumble of the thunder overhead.

Ignoring the fire around him, he twisted around in

mid-flight, struggling to get his feet in front of him like a mountain climber repelling down the side of a cliff.

Bad mistake.

He slammed feet first into the wall, his left leg snapping on impact. White-hot pain ripped through his body. Before he could cry out, the rest of him collided with the concrete.

Black dots tiptoed around the edge of his vision as Griffin lay crumpled on the cold, wet ground; all the nerves in his body misfiring. As his eyesight darkened, he thought he saw a figure separated itself from the wall's shadow and stepped over.

"B-Basil?" With a groan, he raised his head, trying to see.

The figure lifted its foot. "*Basil?*" a cold voice scorned. "Why, not even close." Then the figure stomped down on Griffin's fractured leg, breaking it further.

Stars of pain burst apart in his skull.

Oblivion followed.

* * *

Basil landed with an *oof* in the backyard. One knee buckled slightly from the weight of the figure in his arms. "My apologies, lad," he said when Griffin moaned from the sudden movement.

"Mm-hmm," Griffin said, still half conscious. He kept one arm loosely slung around Basil's neck, blinking groggily as the Mentor made his way cautiously across the yard. The pain from the fractured limb seemed to fill his entire body.

The back door swung open. "What is it with you two?" Sukalli appeared in the doorway, an inky silhouette against the kitchen's light. "Every time I drop by, one of you looks like a leftover from a stampede." He stepped to one side as Basil edged in sideways, mindful of Griffin's injury. "How bad is it?"

"Bad enough." Basil lowered Griffin until the Tiro could stand on one leg next to the table. Pulling out two chairs, he helped Griffin take a seat. He carefully lifted the injured limb and laid it across the other. "Let's see what the damage is."

With gentle hands, he eased off Griffin's shoe and pushed the pant leg up past his knee. He winced. "Broken, to be sure. I'll need to set it before trying to Might-heal it." He started to place his hands upon the injury, then paused and caught Griffin's eye. "Brace yourself."

Griffin swallowed. He held the wooden seat with both hands and gave a nod. Basil took a deep breath, steeling himself. Before he could begin, Sukalli tapped him on the shoulder.

"Let me do that for you." When the Mentor started to protest, Sukalli nudged him aside. "No, brother. Causing your apprentice more pain is a burden you don't need. Go make tea or something." The Guardian took a stance next to Griffin. "All right, pup. I'll try to be as quick as I can." He leaned over and wrapped enormous hands around the leg. "And no bawling like a lost calf," he added with a crooked grin. "Remember, us Earth and Fires are the tough ones."

In spite of the blinding pain, Griffin forced himself to grin back. "True that," he said hoarsely, hoping neither of them noticed the quiver in his voice. He gripped the chair in a white-knuckled hold. "Okay. I'm ready."

Before he could finish the sentence, Sukalli clamped down. Fingers dug into Griffin's calf as his palms pressed down on the both ends of the fractured bone.

In spite of his determination, Griffin cried out. For a moment, the room dimmed around him as the agony tore through his leg and into his gut. He squeezed his eyes tight against the tears. Hands pressed down on his shoulders and held him in place.

Slowly, he became aware of soothing warmth replacing the stabbing pain. He peeked through watering eyes.

Sukalli crouched beside him now, both hands still wrapped around his leg. As Griffin watched, the Guardian shifted to a more comfortable position. He gave a wink.

"You did real good. I'm just about done here."

Griffin nodded and cleared his throat. Bile burned the back of it. He watched as Basil stepped out from behind him and walked over to the storage closet in the corner, the Mentor's face tight with worry. He rummaged around for a few minutes and pulled out a temporary walking cast.

"I hate that thing," Griffin grumbled as Basil handed it to Sukalli. He winced when the Guardian slipped it on and fastened the Velcro straps.

"Give it a test drive, pup."

Griffin swung his leg down off the chair and stood up carefully. He took a timid step and another, then look up at Sukalli. "Fire, you're good. My leg hurts, but it works."

As Griffin took a turn around the kitchen, the walking cast clumping every other step, Sukalli sat down in one of the vacant chairs. "What happened this time?"

Basil took a seat across from him and began describing the mission. "Then the van simply exploded," he finished. "But, I must admit, I was more worried about my Tiro than the safety of the crowd. Luckily, the ambulance and fire department arrived shortly thereafter. In all the commotion, we were able to make good our escape."

Sukalli propped an elbow on the table. "I wonder what made it blow up like that?" He looked over. "Did you notice anything, Griffin?"

Griffin leaned against the counter, leg stuck out in front of him. "No, not really. I mean, all I remember was crashing into the wall and falling to the ground." A vague image danced on the edge of his memory. "Then... then some guy came out the shadows. I thought it was Basil, but then he—"

"How did you know it was a *he*?"

"What?"

"How did you know the figure was male?" Basil asked again.

"He spoke to me. It was a male voice."

"What did he say, little brother?"

Griffin frowned, trying to hold on to the memory. To keep it fixed it in his mind. He squeezed his eyes tight, willing himself to remember.

A sneering voice mocking him.

A foot stomping on his injured leg.

Ice ran up his spine and stiffened the hairs on the back of his neck. Dizziness swamped him as the blood drained from his face. His eyes flew open in recognition.

"Nicopolis." He locked eyes with Basil. "It was Nicopolis.

Chapter Nine

FOR A MOMENT, THE NAME HUNG in the air like a foul stench.

Then, Sukalli banged a fist on the table. Griffin flinched. He winced from the sudden movement.

"I knew it," the Guardian snarled. "I just knew that viper would strike. Sooner than I thought, too."

"Are you saying Nicopolis has caused all our recent *accidents* on mission?" Basil looked skeptically at Sukalli. "How would he be able to arrive ahead of us? Ahead of Flight Command? And to what purpose? Why not just kill us outright?"

Sukalli shook his head. "Aw, you just can't explain crazy. Although he's probably still sane enough to know he's no match for you in a straight-on fight. But until Command can lasso him in, you two are off rotation. Permanently, this time." Ignoring their objections, he rose to his feet. "I'll inform Command. Until then, watch your backs. And legs."

He headed toward the back door, then snapped his fingers. "Almost forgot to tell you why I came by." Toying with his earring, the Earth symbol made from gold wire crafted into a spiral diamond, he thought for a moment. "In fact, the timing couldn't be better. I've just decided that his first assignment is going to be acting as body guard for the two of you. Especially for the pup here. I'll send him over tomorrow morning to work out details with you. He'll be under your command, Basil, since he's a junior Terrae Angelus and you're a Senior Mentor."

"What in heaven's name are you going on about?"

"Why, we've got us an eager young warrior permanently assigned to High Springs, and he's chomping on the bit to show Command what he can do. He's just turned eighteen and promoted from Tiro status."

"Excuse me, but I'm *quite* capable of guarding my own apprentice, thank you very much."

"But not round the clock. So get off your high horse and consider this an order," he added as the Mentor opened his mouth. Basil closed it with poor grace.

"So who is it?" Griffin asked.

Eyes dancing, Sukalli grinned as he answered. "An old compadre of yours."

Griffin frowned in confusion. "I don't know any Tiro who's been promoted..." He let out a groan of recognition when Sukalli nodded. "I don't freaking believe it."

Griffin's Journal: Wednesday, May 25th
Could my life get any worse?
No. Wait. Better not say that.
Because then it always does—especially lately.
And if that jerk makes one comment tomorrow

about my injury, I'm knocking his teeth down his throat. See how he likes eating soup the rest of his life.

I'm just saying.

Basil's Journal: Thursday, May 26th

While I appreciate my old friend's concern, the idea of placing another Terrae Angelus in harm's way to defend me and my Tiro is repugnant. Doesn't Sukalli realize that Nicopolis would have no compunction about killing *him* to get to Griffin and me?

I should have done more than simply punch Nicopolis in the nose.

Something more *permanent*.

While I agree with the ancient philosophy that vengeance belongs only to God, I could be tempted, given the right circumstance, to take matters into my own hands. An eye for an eye.

* * *

Griffin peeked out his bedroom window at the faint thud of something landing on the porch. Squinting into the morning sun, he pressed closer, trying to see, but the roof blocked his view. A moment later, the iron knocker clapped twice. He heard his Mentor inviting someone inside.

"Griffin?" Basil called.

"Do I have to?" He yelled back.

"It will not hurt you to be civil."

Wanna bet? He step-clumped out of the room and

down the stairs.

A figure stood ramrod straight in the entryway. His short hair gleamed almost white, made even whiter in contrast to a black tee shirt and jeans.

Sergei.

He looked up when Griffin appeared on the landing.

"Hey," Griffin muttered after a meaningful look from the Mentor.

"Hey." For a second, Sergei's ice-blue gaze, the same color as Basil's, flicked across the cast.

Griffin's eyes narrowed. *Go ahead*, he thought. *Say something. Anything. Just give me a reason.*

"Guardian Sukalli told me what happened." Sergei nodded toward the brace. "Sorry to hear you got hurt."

Griffin blinked in surprise. "What—no insults? No sarcastic remarks?"

"Well, if you want, I could mock your apparent lack of coordination and second-rate skills. And then you could call me *Ser-jerk*, for old time's sake. Maybe point out my—what was it you said?"

In spite of himself, Griffin's lips twitched. "Your delusions of godhead?"

"Oh, yeah." A smile flitted across Sergei's face for a moment. "You know, that actually was kind of funny."

"Well, shall we talk, then?" Basil led the way through the archway into the living room. Sergei followed. Griffin stumped along after them.

"Congratulations on your rapid promotion." Basil took a seat near the fireplace. Sergei sat down on the sofa while Griffin chose a nearby chair. "Although I am not surprised. Not after seeing you in action."

Sergei tried not to grin at the praise. And failed. "Thank you. And thanks for what you did to help me finish my apprenticeship. I learned a lot from you in the short time we trained together. Working with another Wind and Water really sharpened my skills."

"It usually does. I may have Griffin spend a month or so with another Earth and Fire Mentor when he gets closer to the end of his apprenticeship. Just for that very reason."

"Sukalli?" Griffin guessed.

"No, Guardians do not have the time to work with Tiros. Most likely an old apprentice of mine." He shook his head. "But we're getting ahead of ourselves. Right now, we need to focus on keeping you alive until Nicopolis is no longer a threat."

"I guess that's why I'm here," Sergei said.

"It is. But, as I told Sukalli last night, I am not at all pleased with this arrangement. Do you understand what is going on and the dangers involved?"

"Well, yes," Sergei said. "To some extent. I mean, I know that Nicopolis has been stripped of his rank due to the whole screw up around Griffin's Proelium and what happened afterwards. But, what I don't understand is *why* all this happened in the first place." He leaned forward, arms resting on his knees, and looked at Griffin. "From what Sukalli told me, Nicopolis was your former Mentor, then for some reason, you were assigned to Basil. I guess there's more to that story, right?"

Dread lanced through Griffin. He locked eyes with Basil, hoping his Mentor would pick up the unspoken plea for silence.

"Well, it is quite simple, really," Basil said. "Nicopolis is obviously a raving psychopath with deep seated neurotic tendencies. Or as Griffin so elegantly labels him—a wacko."

With a silent sigh of relief, Griffin sank down in his chair.

"So what's the plan?" Sergei asked.

Basil rested elbows on the arms of the chair and tented his fingertips together as he thought for a minute. He looked from one young face to another. "I cannot believe I am about to propose this, as we all know how well it turned out last time. But I fail to see a more practical solution."

"What do you mean..." Griffin's voice faded as his Mentor's proposal dawned on him. He glared at Sergei. "You have *got* to be kidding. *Him* again?"

"Hey, think how *I* feel," Sergei glared back. "I'll have to share a bathroom with you."

"Don't like it? Then why don't you use the backyard?"

"Why don't you learn to aim?"

"Gentlemen!"

Griffin and Sergei both flinched at the snap in Basil's voice. They turned and looked at him.

"Un-bloody-believable." Basil continued in a quiet voice that fooled neither of them. "There is an insane rogue angel out there, whose one burning desire is murder. While most likely killing any fellow Terrae Angelus who stands in his way. And you two *dunderheads* are sitting there and squabbling about lavatory etiquette." He rose from his seat, face dark with frustration, and headed toward the kitchen. "I am going to brew coffee for us. While I am gone, I want you to settle your petty differences." He paused in the doorway and looked back over a shoulder. "Because whether you like it or not, Team Angel now numbers *three*." He left the room.

For a long minute, they looked everywhere, but at each other. Then, Sergei snorted in disbelief.

"Did he just say *Team Angel?*"

"S'my fault. But you've got to give him credit for trying. You know. At his age." Griffin hesitated, then stood up. Sergei joined him. "So I guess we're going to have to call a ceasefire."

Sergei shrugged. "I guess. But, just so you know— my mission is to keep you and Basil alive. And, I'll do my job to the best of my ability. Which, you have to admit, is freaking phenomenal. But don't expect this truce to make us friends."

Without another word, he walked away toward the kitchen.

Chapter Ten

Sitting On The Edge Of His Bed, Griffin reached down and peeled the straps off the cast with a ripping sound, then tossed it aside. Flexing his leg a few times, he moaned in relief and began limping from one side of the room to the other.

The adjoining bathroom pocket door rumbled when it slid open. Sergei stuck his head around it.

"Okay if I use the same shelf in the cabinet as last time?" He pulled his head back when Griffin gave a nod.

As Griffin took a seat at the desk and powered up his laptop, he listened with one ear to Sergei moving around their shared bathroom. Drawers opened and closed. The ringing of a cell phone in the next room caught his attention.

"Hello? Hey, Dimitri!" Gladness tinged Sergei's voice. "Nope, got here this morning. I'm just finishing unpacking." A long pause. "Yeah, yeah, I'm being careful. But Basil doesn't think Nicopolis is going to try an overt attack. Not with all of us on our guard. I just hope I do okay when push comes to shove." He stopped talking for a minute. "You have to say that—you trained me." A snort of laughter and another long pause. "No, it's fine." Sergei moved from the bathroom into his room; his voice fainter now. "Hey, stop worrying—I'm a big guy now." He laughed again. "No, you just miss me doing all the chores." The door rolled shut on the far side of the bathroom and blocked the rest of the conversation.

Griffin stared blankly at the computer screen as the conversation between Mentor and ex-Tiro reverberated in his head. Leaning back, he swiveled around and stared at the open doorway separating the two rooms. *That could be* me *talking to* Basil.

The computer pinged. Reaching over, he tapped on the e-mail icon and opened the first message. Actually the only message.

He laughed when a picture of Katie, her mouth wide in a silent scream and an enormous pair of fake glasses on her face, appeared. He read the caption. *Just got home from school. Coming over now. By the time you read this, I'll be at your front door.*

Griffin jumped to his feet. His injured leg buckled beneath him. Crying out, he went down, a flailing arm taking out the lamp and sending it flying into the wall. The light bulb exploded with a *pop*. With a booming thud, he crashed to the floor in a heap.

Before he could catch his breath, Sergei burst through the bathroom door, then skidded to a stop when he spied Griffin. "Stay down," he yelled, dropping to one knee next to him. Hands held at the ready, he scanned the room for the enemy.

"It's okay. I just…"

With a mighty blast of Wind, Basil materialized next to them. "Keep back, both of you," he roared. "This is between Nicopolis and…and…" His voice trailed off as he looked around the empty room.

For a moment, all three remained frozen.

Then, Griffin grinned sheepishly. "I, um, tripped." A muted knock came from downstairs. "Oh, that would be Katie."

Basil reached down and grabbed Griffin's arm. Yanking him none too gently to his feet, he pushed him over to the bed. "You—get your brace on." Picking up the device, he handed it to Griffin while he spoke over his shoulder to Sergei. "You—get the door."

"With pleasure." Flashing a smirk from behind Basil's back, Sergei hurried away.

"Tell her I'll be right there," Griffin hollered, sticking his foot into the boot. Fingers fumbled to refasten the straps. Jumping up, he lurched out of the room. Basil followed him.

"Mind the steps," Basil ordered on the way back to his own room. "All we need is for you to break the other leg."

"Yeah, yeah." Griffin hop-stepped as quickly as he could down the stairs. He grinned at the sound of Katie's voice coming from the entryway.

"What do you mean, he broke his leg?" Her voice grew shrill as she continued questioning Sergei. "When? How did it happen? Is he upstairs?"

81

"I'm right here, Katie." He negotiated the final step and joined them in the hall. He kept one hand on the newel post for balance as a slender form in a blue hoodie flung her arms around him.

"Are you okay?" she asked. "What happened? And why is *he* here?"

Griffin noticed she didn't bother to keep her voice down. He hugged her back one-armed. While he filled her in with the events of the last two days, he noticed Sergei loitering nearby. "So, until Nicopolis is no longer a threat, Sergei's here to help us."

Katie took his arm and led him into the living room. They flopped down side by side on the sofa. "Help you? How?"

Sergei hovered in the archway. "Why, I'm his body guard."

"Don't you have to unpack?" Griffin asked pointedly.

"Nope, all done," he said, joining them in the living room. "So, since I've been promoted, they called on me to watch your favorite angels' backs until Flight Command can stop Nicopolis." Taking a stance next to the fireplace, he rested an elbow on the mantle in a perfect pose, and tried not to act like he was flexing his shoulders.

"He's going to get a cramp doing that," Katie muttered under her breath as she leaned forward in the pretense of checking out the walking cast. She straightened and fixed Sergei with a stony look. "By the way, I still think you're a jerk for what you did to Griffin and me."

"Oh, come on. I was just—"

"But I guess I'll let it go. Just make sure you keep him safe. Or Nicopolis will be the least of your problems. Got it?"

"Whoa." Sergei raised both hands in surrender. "I got it."

Grinning at her tough-girl imitation, Griffin nudged her with a elbow. "Maybe I should just keep you around these next few days. Turn *you* loose on Nicopolis next time he shows up."

"Better than taking final exams."

"No doubt. I'd take Nicopolis over Milton anytime."

"Who's Milton?" Sergei asked.

"That algebra teacher from hell."

"Oh, yeah."

"Speaking of which," Katie said. "I need to get back and start studying. I've got science and math finals tomorrow, but then I'm out by noon." She jumped up, keeping one hand on Griffin's shoulder. "No, you stay put." She leaned over for a quick kiss.

Aware of Sergei watching, Griffin made sure he kept the kiss going a bit longer. "Good luck on your finals. Call me when you get done. Since Basil and I are temporarily grounded, we'll be around a lot more."

"Really?" Her blue eyes widened. "Because Cas is having an end-of-year barbeque at his house tomorrow afternoon. Burgers, sodas, volleyball, that sort of thing. He just decided at the last minute to do it. Want to come with me?" She glanced over at Sergei. "I guess you should come, too, and play Secret Service guy."

"I do not believe that would be such a good idea." Basil appeared in the archway. All three looked at the Mentor as he continued. "I'm sorry, but it's much too risky."

"Ah, come on, Basil," Griffin argued. "It's not we're going to be attacked in Cas' backyard."

"And I will be there, just in case," Sergei added.

"Me, too." Katie squared her slender shoulders.

Basil smiled at her. "No doubt you would be formidable in a battle, miss. But I'm afraid my answer is still no." With a polite nod, he turned and headed for the study.

"My life sucks," Griffin muttered under his breath. He pushed himself awkwardly off the sofa and took Katie's hand. "Come on—I'll walk you home. Nah, I can manage," he added as she protested. "My leg's almost healed. The cast is simply for precaution."

As they headed hand-in-hand across the street through the late afternoon, he glanced over at her. "Hey, listen. I want you to go to Cas' party. You shouldn't miss out on good times just because of me."

"I don't know if I want to." She looked down. "I mean, part of the fun of having a boyfriend is being able to do stuff as a couple."

He winced at the sadness in her voice. "I tell you what. I'll find a way to drop by. I'll probably have to bring Ser-jerk along, but at least I could hang with you for awhile."

"I don't like the sound of that. I mean Mr. Raine seemed pretty worried about it. Maybe you should just lay low."

"But don't you see, Katie?" He pulled her to a stop on the sidewalk in front of her house and clasped both her hands in his. "If I start living my life in fear of Nicopolis again, then I'm right back to where I was three years ago. Every minute of every day sick with terror of getting the crap beat out of me." His eyes flashed with a brown fire as he spoke through gritted teeth. "And I am *never* giving him that power over me again."

"Okay," she whispered. Sudden tears sprang to her eyes. "Okay, I get it. But you have to promise me you'll bring Sergei along for protection."

"I promise." He squeezed her hands. "It'll be fine. So look for me tomorrow."

"All right." She smiled through her tears. "And Cas will be happy if you showed up."

Maybe, he thought. *I don't know if I'm still pissed at him or not*. He finished escorting her up the steps to her front door, boot thumping hollowly against the porch's flooring. After another kiss good-bye, this time even longer, he stumped back across the street.

Slipping inside the door, he stuck his head inside the study. He noticed Sergei rummaging through the bookshelf.

"Where's Basil?"

"In the kitchen ordering Chinese take-out for dinner." Sergei pulled out a book and began ruffling through it with a bored air. "Bummer about not getting to go to your little buddy's get-together. Might have even been fun—on a sophomoric level, of course." He looked up in surprise when Griffin closed the door and leaned against it.

"Speaking of the party, I need your help with something," Griffin said. "And I don't want Basil to know about it."

Sergei's eyebrows flew up. "What? I'm stunned. The littlest angel is actually going to try the bad boy routine?"

"Hey, I'm not *that* much of a boy scout. I can be dark and edgy. When I want."

"If you say so." Sergei put the book back on the shelf and rubbed his hands together. "So, what are you planning on doing that Basil can't know about?" His eyes gleamed with anticipation. "Getting a tattoo, right?"

In spite of himself, Griffin grinned. "No, but I've always wanted to. Maybe the symbols of Earth and Fire. One on each shoulder blade."

"Like where celestial angels have their wings?" Sergei blinked in surprise. "That's not a bad idea. I wouldn't mind doing that myself."

For a moment, they looked at each other. Something shifted between them. A crack in the mortar of a stone wall.

They both jumped when Basil tapped on the door and opened it, sending Griffin staggering forward a step. The Mentor paused in the doorway, his gaze darting from one face to another. Suspicion narrowed his eyes.

"What are you two rapscallions up to?"

"Nothing," Sergei said.

"What's a rapscallion?" Griffin asked at the same time.

Basil started to speak when a *rat-tat-tat* sounded from the hall. Both youths scrambled for the door.

"Dinner's here." Griffin dodged around Basil with an awkward lurch.

"Excellent timing—I'm starving." Sergei followed on his heels.

"Oy vey," Basil muttered.

Chapter Eleven

Basil's Journal: Friday, May 27ᵗʰ

YESTERDAY AFTERNOON, SERGEI REJOINED our household to help keep Griffin safe. While I now have *two* to worry about, I must admit it does give me a sense of relief to have another guardian angel around, especially one of Sergei's caliber.

I know their personalities clash (and if that isn't the understatement of the century, I don't know what is), but I hope Griffin noticed that when he fell, Sergei had responded full bore to the perceived threat. He may be arrogant about his abilities and condescending to Griffin, but he is a Terrae Angelus in the most ancient and noble sense of the word.

I believe I can always count on him (and Griffin, for that matter) to do the right thing.

Griffin's Journal: Friday, May 27ᵗʰ

As of yesterday, Sergei's back in our house – that's bad.

As of this morning, I'm done with that stupid brace – that's good.

I have to figure out a way to sneak past Basil to go to a party with Katie – that's bad.

Nicopolis hasn't killed any of us yet – that's good.

When it comes to my life right now, the score is tied.

* * *

With twin *thumps*, Griffin and Sergei materialized behind a tall hedge bordering the Navarre's driveway. Pushing through the branches covered in a fuzz of dainty green leaves, they paused and looked around. Cars covered the wide driveway and lined both sides of the neighborhood street.

Laughing voices and the smell of grilling meat drifted from the Navarre's backyard, filling the late afternoon air. When Griffin started up the driveway, Sergei snagged his arm.

"Wait a sec. Since I'm supposed to be your cousin, you better fill me in on who's who and all that."

"Oh, yeah. That would help with our cover story." Griffin held up his hand and begin ticking off with his fingers. "Cas Navarre. Fellow sophomore and friend of Katie and mine. We met when I was going to school for those few weeks I was mortal. His dad, James Navarre, is a school counselor at Centennial High. His mom, Sylvia Navarre, is a nurse, and Tessie is their little girl."

Sergei's face fell. "How little?"

"Young enough to still recognize who and what we really are. Luckily, they all think it just a phase or something."

"At least they don't have a dog."

With a wave of his hand, Griffin led the way around the house and into the backyard. For a moment, they stood unnoticed as several dozen high school students milled around. Most of them held paper plates and soda cans, while a few tried to keep a volleyball game going at one end of the yard.

A high pitched squeal jerked their heads toward the brick patio near the house. A tiny form in yellow overalls hurtled toward them as fast as her legs could run.

"Gwiffin," Tessie cried as she raced toward him.

"*Gwiffin?*" Delight flooded Sergei's face.

"Shut up." Ignoring the other Terrae Angelus' chortle of glee, Griffin braced himself. Tessie barreled into him and flung her arms around his knees. She tilted her head back, wisps of dark hair framing her round face, and smiled up in adoration at him. As she began babbling nonstop to him about something that sounded like puppies or guppies, he reached down and untangled her arms.

"Tessie, take a breath and tell me where Cas is."

Grabbing his hand, she started to pull him across the yard. She paused when she noticed Sergei behind him.

"Oooh." She let go and pranced over on tiptoes to Sergei. Her soft brown eyes widened as she gazed up at him. "'Nother angel," she whispered in growing delight.

"Tessie, this is Sergei." A wicked expression spread across Griffin's face. "Can you say Sergei?"

"Suh-gee," she crowed.

"That's right, Tessie. This is *Suh-gee*." Griffin patted her on her head. "That's my girl. Now, take me to Cas."

Tugging on his hand, Tessie led him over to the far corner of the yard where smoke billowed from the grill. Sergei followed on their heels.

"Hey, Raine!" Cas appeared from within a cloud, waving a spatula. He handed it to another student. "Here, finish flipping the patties for me." He walked over with a happy expression.

At the sight of his friend, Griffin found himself smiling back, the residual resentment fading away. He aimed a punch at his friend's stomach and laughed when Cas blocked it. They bumped fists.

"How it's going, Cas?"

"School is done. Summer is here. And an old friend showed up." Cas grinned. "Life is sweet."

"Where's your folks. I wanted to say hi to them, especially your dad."

"They ran to the store for more of, well, everything." His brown eyes squinted in curiosity at the figure behind Griffin.

"Cas, this is Sergei. The cousin I told you about?"

Sergei stepped forward. "You might know me as Ser-jerk."

Cas' mouth sagged open in surprise at Sergei's admission. Before he could recover, another boy shouted at Cas to come check the burgers. When he stepped away, Tessie slid closer to Sergei and patted his knee, trying to get his attention.

"Suh-gee?" She pointed a pudgy finger at Griffin. "Bwother? Gwiffin bwother?"

Sergei gazed down at Tessie. An odd expression softened his handsome face. "Well, yeah, I guess we are. In a way." He glanced up. Seeing Griffin watching, he curled his lip. "Of course, I'm the smarter brother. The more talented and better looking brother."

At that moment, Katie emerged from the house, her friend, Carlee, in tow. Spying Griffin and Sergei, they hurried over and joined them, Carlee's red curls bouncing with every exuberant step. After introducing Carlee and Sergei to each other, Katie turned to Griffin.

"Is everything okay?" she asked in an undertone. "How did you guys get past Basil?"

Griffin led her a few feet away toward the back door standing ajar. "Sergei and I picked a fight with each other. I pretended to storm off to my room to sulk. Then Sergei said that he was going for a walk to cool off. This was all after Basil said he didn't want to see either of us for a few hours until we both had a chance to simmer down and discuss our differences like gentlemen," he said in a perfect imitation of the Mentor's British accent. "So we can hang out for about an hour, then we better get back." He peered into her face. "Sorry I can't stay longer."

"Hey, I'm just glad you're here, even for a little while." Katie glanced past his shoulder and grinned. "And, apparently, so is Carlee. She's flirting like mad with Sergei and talking a mile a minute. Oh, look. He's backing up, trying to make a break for it." Griffin turned to watch.

With a shriek like a soul in torment, a gale of wind suddenly slammed into the yard.

Fire shot up from the grill in a roar, igniting the hamburger patties, and sending them flaming into the air. Girls squealed when paper plates flipped upside down and landed on their laps. In the corner of the yard, the volleyball net ripped loose from one of the poles and whipped around, flailing the players. A boy standing to one side of the court screamed. He crumbled to the ground, cupping a hand over his face.

"Fire!" Griffin cursed, then grabbed Katie and pushed her through the open door into the house. "Stay inside," he ordered. "No matter what!"

Bent over, he hurried toward Sergei and the others still in the far corner. The wind picked up with every step he took. Clouds boiled overhead and darkened the sky; flashes of lightening yellowed their underbellies. Paper plates, hamburger buns, and soda cans hurled through the air like shrapnel. The other teens buffeted him as they surged toward the house for safety, the building half hidden by flying rubbish. With another clap of thunder, the clouds split open. Rain began pounding down in a cold torrent.

Squinting, he spied Sergei half hidden in the center of what looked like a small tornado. The Terrae Angelus stood with legs braced apart, both arms extended out from his sides as wind and debris churned around him. At his feet, Cas hunkered down, his body folded over his sister, shielding her from the storm's fury; blood trickled from a cut on his forehead. Tucked between her brother's knees, Tessie's mouth stretched wide open as she wailed, her cries drowned out by the wind.

Understand flashed through Griffin's mind. *By the Light! He's creating a vortex to protect them*, he thought. *Like the eye of the hurricane.* "Fire, he *is* good."

Still keeping low, Griffin scurried over to the three-some. He rose to his feet as Sergei dropped his arms, chest heaving. Along with Cas and Tessie, both angels were soaked by the pouring rain.

"Where's Carlee?" Griffin yelled over the wind, his wet hair half blinding him.

"She bolted to the house already," Sergei gasped. "Take the baby. I'll get Cas."

Griffin nodded. Squatting down, he reached for Tessie. "Let me carry her, Cas. Sergei's going to help you get inside." Without hesitation, Cas thrust his sobbing sister into Griffin's arms. "I'll be right behind you," he reassured his friend.

Cas nodded, wiped the blood from his brow, then lurched to his feet. Sergei grabbed his arm as he staggered.

"Here. Let me help with that cut," the Terrae Angelus yelled in Cas's ear. Placing a hand on the boy's forehead, he effectively covered his eyes. Before Cas could move, Sergei disappeared, taking the teen with him.

Cas'll never know what just happened. "Okay, our turn," Griffin said, nestling the child's wet face into his

94

neck. He patted her back. "Want to go for a ride, Tessie?" He frowned when she stiffened in his arms and stared over his shoulder.

Her scream pierced the storm.

Instinct drove Griffin to his knees just as the picnic table shot past, missing their heads by less than an inch. It crashed into the back wall of the yard. Pieces of splintered wood soared into the air straight toward them like spears.

Pumping his legs, Griffin launched himself toward the house with everything he had. With the child clasped against his chest, he vanished.

Reality stilled when the silent, silvery mistiness of flight, as if they were inside a cloud, enveloped them. Tessie gasped with delight, her mouth a perfect O.

"I know." Griffin whispered in her ear. "Flying is *way* cool."

A moment later, they materialized with a thump outside the door. As he reached for the knob, it flew open. Sergei stood on the other side.

"You guys okay?" he said over the hum of voices. The other teens packed the kitchen. Water dripped from their clothing. Several boys laughed as they wrung out their tee shirts, adding to the puddles on the floor. A few decided not to put them back on, to the delight of some of the girls.

"All good." Griffin set Tessie down. He looked around the crowded room for Katie. Relief swept through him when he spotted her next to the sink dabbing the blood from Cas' forehead. She said something to the boy, who turned around.

Tessie? Cas mouthed.

Griffin gave a thumbs up and pointed toward his feet. He grinned when Tessie began snaking her way through the forest of legs toward her brother.

"Hey." Sergei nudged Griffin to get his attention. "Was it Nicopolis?"

"Had to be. And I think Tessie spotted him." A sickening horror squirmed in his gut at the thought of Nicopolis close by. Near Katie and the Navarre family.

Sergei frowned while he scanned the room, blonde hair darkened from the rain. "They're all in danger while we're here. And if I have to battle that guy, I don't want to do with a bunch of mortals around. We better take off."

"Right." Catching Katie's eye over the heads of the milling crowd, he pointed to his watch and waved good-bye. He grinned when she blew him a farewell kiss.

Next to her, Cas made a gagging motion. In mock indignation, Katie punched him on the arm. He laughed and bent over to pick up Tessie, plopping his little sister down on the counter between him and Katie. Pulling a wad of paper towels from the dispenser, Katie began drying the child's face and hair.

Griffin watched from across the room as Katie and Cas continued to tease each other over Tessie's head. For a moment, it felt like he was standing outside a window and looking in.

He blinked when someone jostled his arm.

"We're leaving. Now," Sergei said in a low voice. "He'll follow us home and leave them alone. Plus..." He left the rest unspoken.

Griffin nodded in understanding. "Plus, Basil will be there. A one angel NORAD." Drying his sweaty hand on his jeans, he took hold of the doorknob. "You ready?"

"Go low and to the left," Sergei ordered. "When you take off, make your trajectory as vertical as you can. Then kick for home with everything you got."

"What about you?"

"I'll be right behind you covering your butt. So make sure you don't pass gas or something."

Griffin snorted. The trepidation within him eased for a split second. Careful to avoid looking at Katie and Cas, he glanced once more around the room and took a deep breath.

Yanking the door open, he flung himself into the storm.

Chapter Twelve

HEAD DOWN, GRIFFIN SCURRIED across the patio. He flinched when the lightning cracked above the house as if spotting him. Pausing, he squinted over a shoulder. Several steps behind, Sergei waved him on with an impatient gesture.

"Move, move," he shouted over the storm.

Bending his knees until they touched his chest, Griffin gave a grunt as he launched himself into the squall. A split second later, Sergei followed. As they vanished into the air, the rain faded to a drizzle, then stopped. Sunlight broke through as the clouds rolled away.

Following them.

Hunting them.

* * *

"Griffin?" Waiting by the bottom step for a response, Basil drummed his fingers against the newel post. "Griffin, I'm not calling you again," he shouted again, voice rising in vexation.

Silence filled the house.

The Mentor frowned. Then comprehension swept

through him. *I don't believe it—he went to the party after all*, he thought. *Well, he's going to be mightily embarrassed when I haul him home by the scruff of the neck. And if Sergei had any part of this, he's going to get an earful, too.*

"Bloody teenagers." With a growl of frustration, he took a step and vanished.

* * *

Coming in too fast, Griffin belly-flopped into the middle of the backyard and skidded a few yards across the wet grass. Gasping for air, he rolled over, wiped the muck from his face, and scrambled to his feet. With a *whoosh*, fireballs ignited in his cupped hands. Taking a defensive posture, he shook dripping hair out of his face, lips tight as he scanned the cloudy sky above him.

Come on, dude, he thought. *You were right behind me.*

Thunder belched out a drawn out rumble overhead. As it died away, curse words began filling the air from an unseen source. A moment later, Sergei materialized by the back wall, clothes plastered against him from both the rain and flight. Blue eyes blazing, he stalked toward Griffin.

"What were you doing back there—sucking your thumb?" He poked a finger into Griffin's chest. "I told you full throttle and you slowed down halfway home."

Clenching his fists, Griffin extinguished his Fire and yelled back. "I know what I'm doing—it's not my first rodeo with that monster. Plus, I wanted to make sure you were okay."

Sergei pushed his face into Griffin's. "Next time I tell you to move your ass," he growled, "move your ass. Or it'll get kicked."

"Don't order me around—you're not my Mentor!"

They both whirled around at a snigger.

Nicopolis stood in the far corner of the yard, his gray suit mirroring the sky. With a wave of a hand, the storm abated; to the west, the setting sun peeked out from below the clouds.

"Oh, that's better." Nicopolis smoothed a lock of thin pale hair across his forehead, then plucked a crisply folded piece of material from his breast pocket and patted the moisture from his face. "There. All clean and tidy." He looked Griffin up and down as he tucked the handkerchief away. "Pity I can't say the same about you. You're still the disgusting little Earth and Fire reject I remember."

Griffin's pulse began to race as memories clawed at him. He fought to ignore them. "What the hell do you want?"

"Such language. Is that anyway to speak to a Mentor?" Nicopolis snapped his fingers. "Oh. Wait. I stand corrected." His pallid lips twisted like worms. "Thanks to you, that designation no longer applies to me."

Griffin willed himself to lock eyes with his former Mentor. "It wasn't my fault. You did it to yourself," he said, silently furious at his unsteady voice.

Nicopolis tilted his head to one side. "Oh, do I detect a quiver in your voice? Can it be you still *fear* me?

As well you should. All those beatings were not a complete waste of time, then. Maybe you did, indeed, learn something at my hand."

Out of the corner of an eye, Griffin spied movement. Sergei stepped forward and took a stance next to him.

With a sneer, Nicopolis shifted his attention. "And you must be Sergei. Formerly apprenticed to Dimitri, and now serving as this one's body guard." He nodded at their surprised expressions. "Oh, yes, I've heard all about you. *Tsk, tsk.* How degrading it must be for a Wind and Water with your skills and reputation to be reduced to nanny. Yet another example of how low we've sunk." He shook his head and motioned for Sergei to step aside. "This has nothing to do with you, so run along and play guardian angel for someone else."

Sergei ignored him. "Go get Basil," he said to Griffin, his gaze never leaving the ex-Mentor.

"Oh, please." Nicopolis gave a snort. "Do not insult my intelligence. Basil is obviously not home, or he would be with us right now, all swollen with righteous anger and fulfilling his role of protective father-figure. Am I right?"

Griffin and Sergei looked at each other as the fact sunk in. Then, tightening his jaw, Griffin raised his chin. "Guess we'll have to handle you ourselves. Of course, two against one is hardly fair, but hey, life sucks that way sometimes."

"Or we could flip a coin," Sergei said to Griffin. "Winner gets to kick the crap out of him and the loser has to buy the pizza."

"Great idea. Remember to tip the driver when you pay."

Nicopolis made an impatient gesture. "Your adolescent bantering is becoming tiresome." He looked at Griffin, eyes dead fish flat. "Now, you and I have unfinished business. And, if you do not wish for your friend to get hurt, I suggest you tell him to leave."

Griffin hesitated before speaking out of the corner of his mouth. "Listen, Sergei. Maybe you *should* take off. Find Basil and—"

"What, and miss all the fun?" Sergei interrupted him with a laugh. "Nah, I think I'll stick around."

Nicopolis shrugged. "As you wish. Actually, this works out quite well for me—I've been eager to practice using my new *acquisition* on a test subject." He pulled out something from a pocket and held it up. A flat, circular pendant, with an open design and crafted from gray stone, dangled from a chain. "Curious how things work out. I thought my exile to the Middle East was a punishment. When, in fact, it was my salvation." Holding up the pendant to one eye like a monocle, he peered through it and cackled. "Look what I discovered there."

"You're right," Sergei said. "This guy's a total loony tune."

Griffin nodded in agreement. "So," he said to Nicopolis. "You found some jewelry that goes with your suit. Nice. But what does that have to do with us?"

"Why, *everything*, you ignoramus." Nicopolis slipped

the chain around his neck and pointed at the object. "So insignificant, and yet so potent. And while you two would have no idea what *this* is, your Mentors would. They would cower in fear from the power contained in my little treasure."

"What do you mean? What kind of power?" Sergei asked.

Nicopolis swelled with delight. "Why, God-like power," he said, and pointed a finger.

A blast of Wind knocked Griffin off his feet. He flew backwards and crashed against the side of the house, rattling the kitchen window. The impact drove the air out of his lungs. For a long minute he laid there struggling to breath. Shouts echoed faintly around him. Finally, he braced a hand against the wall and pushed himself upright, vision blurry. He blinked, trying to clear it. "Oh, no," he whispered.

In the corner of the yard next to the stone wall, Sergei laid crumbled on one side, unconscious. Blood trickled down the side of his face from a gash on his scalp. Nicopolis bent over him, one hand clutching the pendant.

"Hmm," the ex-Mentor said in a matter-of-fact voice. "This isn't working very well. It appears I'll need more practice." He started to place his palm on the younger angel's chest.

With a gasp, Griffin pushed off the wall and staggered forward. "Leave him alone."

Nicopolis straightened. "Or what?" He took a step

toward Griffin. "You'll shoot some feeble little streams of Fire at me? Hardly a threat. Remember, I've seen your pathetic attempts at Element control before and—"

"Oh, shut up," Griffin muttered, then thrust out a hand. Fire exploded from the tips of his fingers.

Caught off guard with the force and fury of flame, Nicopolis flung up an arm and with a howl stumbled backwards just in time. Rage darkened his features. "How dare you!" He took another step forward, then vanished. A second later, he re-appeared in front of Griffin. Eyes blazing with madness, he seized him around the throat.

The strength of the ex-Mentor's Might shocked Griffin. He tore at the hands encircling his neck. Nicopolis squeezed harder. In desperation, he dug thumbs under his assailant's fingers, trying to loosen the hold. Snarling, the ex-Mentor squeezed even harder and forced Griffin to his knees, bending the Tiro's head back.

"Look what you have driven me to," Nicopolis spat, breath sour. "I was once a respected Terrae Angelus. On the fast track to becoming a Guardian. But, thanks to you, I am nothing. *Nothing!*" He tightened his grip, then leaned closer until they were almost nose-to-nose. "So I have nothing to lose by killing you."

Clawing at Nicopolis' wrists, Griffin's lungs began to burn from lack of oxygen. Black spots danced around the edges of his eyes. As his vision narrowed to only Nicopolis' face, it felt like he was looking down a dark tunnel into hell. Nicopolis' gloating visage faded away when red-tinged murkiness enveloped him. A low note hummed in his ears. It deepened and turned into a voice, speaking softly.

Suddenly, Griffin was thirteen again. Sitting up in bed, arms clasped around his knees, unable to sleep because of nightmares. Listening while Basil, seated at the foot of the mattress, read aloud the ancient words to help calm nerves and chase away fears; the Mentor's voice an anchor.

"*For we wrestle not against flesh and bone,* Basil had read, *but against principalities, against powers, against the rulers of the darkness of this world, against spiritual wickedness in high places. Wherefore take unto you the whole armor of God, that ye may be able to withstand the evil day, and having done all, to stand.*'"

Might welled up in Griffin's chest. The power surged outward in a flood, singing through his body like a chorus of angels, to the tips of fingers and toes. His eyes snapped open. Grabbing Nicopolis' arms, he ripped free. With a *whoop,* he sucked in a breath, then staggered to his feet and shoved with both hands.

Nicopolis flew backwards, arms flapping like broken wings. He landed with a grunt a few yards away. As the ex-Mentor lurched upright, Griffin ignited one fireball after another, and hurtled them toward his enemy.

Nicopolis slapped frantically at the fiery missiles. He started to speak, then jerked his head up. Eyes narrowed, he stared into the sky, mouth twisting in hatred. In a gust of Wind, he vanished.

Chapter Thirteen

A second later, Basil blasted into the yard. Relief turned Griffin's legs to rubber bands. He sank to the ground. "About time," he rasped.

"By the Light!" The Mentor raced over to him and knelt down. "How badly are you hurt?"

Griffin winced from the pain of a bruised throat. "Sergei first," he croaked, pointing to the motionless figure near the wall.

Patting him on the shoulder, Basil nodded. "Stay put."

He watched while Basil hurried across the yard. Reaching Sergei, he dropped to one knee and rolled him over onto his back. The younger angel groaned and blinked awake.

"Crap, that hurts!" Sergei said, making a face as he touched the wound. With Basil's help, he sat up and looked around. "Is Griffin okay?"

Griffin gave him a thumbs up. Sergei nodded his thanks when Basil pulled him to his feet. After stopping to collect Griffin, the three made their way inside.

Griffin and Sergei collapsed on kitchen chairs as Basil bustled about gathering ice packs and the first aid kit. After seeing to their various injuries, the Mentor prepared hot tea for all. Taking a seat across from them, he cradled a steaming mug in his hands.

"I should reprimand you two severely for that stunt you pulled—and believe me, I will later—but first I need to know what happened."

Holding a square of gauze to his head, Sergei began, recounting the events up until he was knocked unconscious. Griffin took up the tale, voice still hoarse from the attack. His eyes opened wide at the Mentor's next question.

"This pendant Nicopolis was making a fuss about," Basil asked. "What did it look like?"

"Like a flat, heavy ring of stone, about the size of a silver dollar," Griffin said. "It had four nubs sticking out around the outer edge on the cardinal points. Like on a compass."

"Would you draw it for me?"

Griffin rose and stepped over to the drawer next to the telephone. Grabbing a pad and pencil, he sat back down and sketched for a minute. He pushed it over.

Basil stiffened as he studied the drawing. Without a word, he tore the sheet off the pad and tucked it into a shirt pocket. Before Griffin could ask, he shook his head. "I'll need to show this to Sukalli." Changing the subject, he turned to Sergei. "And how is the head? I'm surprised Nicopolis was able to handle the two of you with such apparent ease. Especially you, Sergei."

"Hey, I was distracted by what he was saying, that's all. He just got the drop on me." Sergei looked at Griffin, a question in his eyes. "What did he mean by *all those beat*—"

"Do you think he's going to try something again?" Griffin interrupted, face turning red. He sighed in relief when Sergei dropped the subject.

"Undoubtedly," Basil said. "And since Nicopolis demonstrated a blatant disregard for the lives and safety of mortals, we'll need to change our strategy. As much as I detest fleeing from an enemy, it might be wise if we went into hiding. At least until Command has captured him."

"What are they going to do to him once they catch him?" Griffin asked.

Basil didn't answer. Instead, he rose and plucked the phone from its cradle on the wall. After punching in the numbers, he waited for the connection, eyes gazing into the distance. "I wish Lena were still with us. I could use her advice and expertise more than ever."

A lump formed in Griffin's throat, both the sound of the grief in Basil's voice as well as the sense of loss in his heart. He swallowed, trying to force it down.

Dropping the ice pack on the table, Sergei leaned over. "Listen. I, um, didn't get a chance earlier to say I was sorry to hear about Miss Weiss passing away. I know she and Basil worked together for a long time."

Griffin cleared his throat, careful to keep his eyes fixed somewhere around Sergei's left ear. "Yeah, thanks."

"Ah, good evening, Howard." The Mentor leaned back against the counter as he spoke into the phone. "Basil here." He blinked in surprise. "No, Basil the Terrae Angelus." His mouth tightened. "Yes, I'll hold." A minute passed. And another. "Well, I'm relieved you found the file. Yes, it is rather thick, but I am quite sure—" He stopped and raised an eyebrow. "An audit?" The other eyebrow went up. "Of my expenses?" Closing his eyes, he ran a hand down his face as he listened. "Well, of course, I spend that much each week on food—I have a sixteen year old apprentice. No, I do not think four gallons of milk are extreme." He shook his finger in silent admonishment when Griffin stifled a laugh. "Yes, I'm well aware of the high cost of salmon, but the lad cannot eat meat, so—" Basil paused, then spoke again through gritted teeth. "Look, Howard, while I appreciate your enthusiasm in monitoring the Foundation's cash flow, I do have an emergency situation here. Can we discuss this at another time? Much obliged." In a clipped tone, he explained what he needed and hung up. "Bloody piker," he muttered under his breath.

"Probably not the time to ask for an upgrade on my cell phone," Griffin said.

"Not if you wish to continue to eat." Basil shook his head. "Well, while Howard makes the necessary arrangements, you two need to pack. Bring clothes for mountain conditions and enough for several weeks. Plus both your laptops, cell phones, and any books you might want. Sergei, please do not contact Dimitri. I want to keep this move as secret as possible. Once we're away, we'll get word to him so he won't worry." He smiled knowingly. "Yes, I realize you're no longer his Tiro, but he would appreciate knowing what is going on, nonetheless." Sergei gave a nod and left the room. Basil turned to Griffin. "You and I are going over to the Heflins. They need to be aware of the recent events, and you'll want to say goodbye to Katie."

"I really don't like the idea of running away from that creep. Can't we deal with him here?"

"I'm afraid not. Plus, the Heflins will be safer without us around."

A few minutes later, they knocked on the Heflins' front door. A booming bark echoed from the other side. Helen Heflin's voice followed, ordering the dog back as she opened the door.

"I thought it must be you from Bear's happy dance," she said with a smile, pale hair and blue eyes a match of her daughter's. She staggered a step as Bear crowded past to lick both the Terrae Angeli's hands in turn.

Griffin paused in the entryway to ruffle the dog's ears as Helen and Basil continued on into the living room. He knelt down and took Bear's long head between his hands. Gazing into eyes the same shade of brown as his, he leaned closer and whispered.

"Listen, big guy, I'm going to be gone for awhile. Maybe for a long time. So I want you to watch over Katie for me, okay?" Bear wagged his tail, eager to please. "You'll be like a giant, furry guardian angel." Griffin wrinkled his nose when the dog licked his face. "With bad breath." He wrapped his arms around the dog's neck and gave him a hug. With a final pat, he rose and joined the other.

Lewis Heflin glanced up from a seat on the sofa next to his wife as Griffin walked in. "Katie's fine, son. She got home a little while ago and told us what happened. Why don't you go on upstairs." He gave Griffin a wink and turned his attention back to Basil as the Mentor continued explaining.

Nodding his thanks, Griffin left and headed for the stairs. Taking them two at a time, he sped up as he spotted Katie rushing out of her bedroom. Meeting in the upper corridor, Katie threw herself into his arms.

For a long minute, Griffin held her, breathing in the vanilla scent of her hair still damp from a shower. He could feel her heart beating against his chest; he hugged her tighter at the sound of sniffles.

"Hey, don't cry," he whispered as she burrowed her face into his neck, her tears wetting his skin. "I'm all in one piece." Patting her back, he asked. "Are Cas and Tessie okay?"

Katie pulled back, tears still clinging to her eyelashes. "Yeah, everyone is fine. They all think it was just a sudden bad storm. Cas just had a scratch. Tessie cried a little after you left, but then she settled down when Mr. and Mrs. Navarre got home." She wiped her face. "Was it...*him*?"

"We need to talk." Taking her hand, Griffin led her

back into the bedroom, mindful of keeping the door open. They shoved the ever-present pile of clothes to one side and took a seat on the rumpled cover. He glanced around. "Don't you *ever* clean?"

"No, and you're stalling for time."

"How do you know that?"

"Because, Angel Boy, I can read you like a cheap paperback." She wrapped cold fingers around his hand. "Right now, you are trying to figure out how to tell me that you and Basil and Sergei are leaving. For everyone's safety. And you don't know when you'll be back or even if you can contact me."

"H-how did you know all that?"

"Why, I eavesdropped, of course. I overheard Basil talking to Mom and Dad right before you came up-stairs." She raised her chin. "So, I'm going to be brave and not get all girly, as you call it, when you leave." Biting down on her trembling lip before it could betray her, she added. "So, get this over with as fast as you can, okay?"

Griffin nodded, unable to speak for a moment. He cleared his throat with a wince. "You know, I thought we'd be spending this summer together doing stuff. But things are going to be crazy for awhile." He squeezed her hand and forced himself to continue with the decision he had made earlier. "So, I think you should hang out with Cas. If you want." He shook his head as Katie began protesting. "No, listen, please. He's a good friend to both of us, and I'd feel better knowing you and him are...you know...not alone."

"Griffin? We need to leave," Basil called from below.

"I'll meet you out front," he yelled back. He stood and pulled Katie to her feet. Guiding her over to the window, he positioned her in front of it and took a stance behind her. A star winked at them in dusky blue sky. "Look,' he said, pointing to it. "The first star. Close your eyes when you make a wish. That way, it always comes true."

"Always?"

"Always and forever."

"Promise?"

"I promise," Griffin whispered. As Katie squeezed her eyes tight, he took a step back.

And vanished.

Chapter Fourteen

Griffin's Journal: Saturday, May 28th

The only way for me to stop thinking about Katie is to keep busy.

Busy staying alive.

It's two in the morning, and I just finished packing. Well, not packing as much as throwing a bunch of stuff in my duffle and my book bag. Mostly, I loaded supplies from the kitchen into boxes. I don't see how all our stuff is going to fit in the Saab. Especially with three of us.

I wonder where we're going?

Basil's Journal: Saturday, May 28th

In all the centuries I have been on Earth, I've never had to flee before an enemy. It galls me now to do so. Hopefully, Command will capture Nicopolis sooner than later, and we can all return to our regular lives. When I spoke with Sukalli earlier about the attack, he informed me that Command is making the hunt for Nicopolis their number one priority.

It's about bloody time.

Howard should be here shortly. God give me patience. He means well, but...

* * *

"Well, Howard, that is certainly larger than my Saab." Basil stood on the lowest step of the porch examining the massive vehicle parked on the street in front of their house. Its dark green color looked almost black in the glow of the streetlight.

"Technically, the Saab belongs to the Foundation, not you personally," Howard murmured absently as he flipped open a ledger and made a mark on the first sheet. He handed it to Basil. "You'll need to sign here for the Jeep," he said, pointing to the bottom of the page. As Basil scribbled his signature, Howard glanced around. "How long will you and your apprentice be away?"

"As long as it takes." Basil looked over as Griffin appeared in the doorway. "Ah, there you are." He gestured for him to join them. "Howard, this is my Tiro, Griffin. Griffin, this is Mr. Howard Needle, our new liaison with the Foundation."

"Sir." Griffin nodded once and held out his hand to the pudgy man.

Mr. Needle shook it, his double chin wobbling along with the gesture. "How rare—manners in a teenager. Lena Weiss was right about you. My condolences on your loss."

Social rituals concluded, he turned back to Basil and handed him a large, thick manila envelope. "A map and all the information you need is in here, along with some cash. Additional funds have been transferred into your account, as well as Griffin's. I assume you will monitor his spending?"

"Of course. I will keep him out of the malt shop and record store."

"What's a record?" Griffin asked.

"Sadly, an anachronism." Basil dug into a pocket and handed the Saab's key to Mr. Needle. "Thank you for doing all this at such short notice. Here's your ride back."

Needle ignored the proffered key. "And I do ask that you keep all receipts and a report of your expenses."

"Right," Basil said with a tight smile. "Well, thank you again. I won't keep you another minute. Time is money, after all."

Finally taking both the hint and the key, Needle nodded goodbye and waddled over to the sports car. After several minutes of adjusting the seat, checking the mirrors, he inched backwards out of the driveway and drove off. The Saab's rumble faded into the distance.

Griffin sighed. "I miss Miss Lena. For lots of reasons."

"As do I, lad."

* * *

Basil winced as the top of his head collided against the interior roof of the Jeep. He rubbed his scalp and glanced over at the driver. "Could you have taken that cattle guard a little faster?"

"Probably." Griffin shrugged as he bounced through

a pothole. The dust from the narrow mountain road billowed up behind them, amber-colored from the light of the morning sun. He swerved to avoid a suicidal chipmunk and cursed under his breath, eyes red-rimmed from lack of sleep.

Basil raised an eyebrow, but said nothing. He shifted, trying to find another inch of room in the passenger seat, grateful for a break from driving. Giving up, he gazed out the window at the surrounding mountains covered in pines and aspens, eyes thoughtful. After a few minutes, he glanced over a shoulder into the backseat at the figure slumped against the side door. "He's still asleep, I see."

"I wish," Sergei grumbled, eyes closed. "But somebody, who totally sucks at driving, keeps hitting every bump." He opened his eyes and rocked the driver's seat in front of him with both knees. "It's called a steering wheel because you're supposed to *steer* around things."

"Hit my seat again," Griffin said with a glare at the rearview mirror, "and I'm pulling over."

"Why? Do you have to take *another* piss? I swear— we'd make better time if you just wore a diaper."

Before he could stop himself, Griffin made a gesture over his shoulder involving a single digit. He winced when Basil reached across and flicked him on the ear. Hard.

"Do that again, Tiro, and I'm strapping you onto the roof for the rest of our journey." He looked back at Sergei. "And you—stop baiting him." Resting his head against the seat rest, he closed his eyes. "Gentlemen, I realize you two are both short-tempered from worry and exhaustion, but really? Is this the time for such childish behavior?"

"He started it," they said simultaneously.

Eyes still shut, Basil pointed a finger at his temple and mimicked pulling a trigger.

* * *

Forty minutes later, Griffin slowed to a crawl at Basil's command. The Mentor consulted the map spread across his lap.

"Hmm, it should be...*there*." He pointed toward a small, wooden arrow nailed to a convenient dead pine, the tree's upper half burned away from an old lightning strike. The arrow pointed to an even narrower dirt driveway snaking away westward through a thick stand of aspens.

Navigating around more rocks and holes, they came out the other side of the grove and found themselves at the edge of a large valley, almost a half mile across. On either side of it, mountains rose to the north and south, while directly ahead, the morning sun highlighted the pass to the west.

Tucked off to one side of the vale sat a two-story lodge, crafted from mammoth logs and complete with a deep front porch. Its large front door was flanked by generous windows on either side. Beyond the structure, a stream emptied into a pond before splashing over a beaver's dam on the opposite side.

They continued down the road toward the lodge. Wheeling into a graveled area off one side of the building, Griffin parked, then turned off the engine. Sniffing the air, he stuck his head out the open window and peered upward.

"Welcome to our home for the next few weeks," Basil said. "Isolated, but quite grand, I would say."

"I don't know about isolated." Griffin gestured toward the white wisp curling from the cabin's massive stone chimney. "I thought I smelled smoke. Looks like someone's here." He glanced at Basil. "Were you expecting anyone?"

"Whoever it is," Sergei said, stretching his back with a pop. "I hope they made breakfast. I'm starving."

Before Basil could answer, the front door opened. All three of them tensed when a large figure appeared. The figure stepped out of the shadows and paused on the front step, bronze face lit by the morning sun.

"About time you got here," Sukalli called. "I thought I'd have to eat all these flapjacks by myself."

Groaning with anticipation, Griffin jumped out, followed by Sergei. They hurried across the lawn and jogged up the steps. Basil followed, a bag in one hand.

"Heard you two had a run-in with our local loco." Sukalli studied them with a sharp expression. "Held your own, too, I hear."

"Well, kind of," Griffin admitted. His stomach growled.

Sukalli gestured toward the open door. "Breakfast is on the table." He stepped to one side as Sergei darted inside with Griffin on his heels.

"Thank you, my friend, for meeting us here." Basil sighed as he walked up the steps. He paused and turned to gaze around the valley. "In my wildest dreams, I would have never predicted Nicopolis would descend so far into the proverbial pit."

"Command will find him—I'll personally see to that."

"And then what? Imprisonment? Or worse?"

Sukalli shook his head, black ponytail swaying from side to side. "We'll ford that river when we come to it. Right now, we need to concentrate on two things. Keeping you all safe and hunting that snake down."

"In all our long history, we have never had to lock away or execute one of our own. How can we start now?" Remorse clouded Basil's voice.

"You know, Mayla has a different outlook on all this—one that you might want to ponder."

"And that is?"

"She believes karma will decide Nicopolis' fate.

Chapter Fifteen

"This place is a joke," Sergei said. He stood in the middle of the great room and looked around. "It's like all the T.V. westerns from the fifties came here to die."

Griffin joined him. "No kidding. Check those out." He pointed up at the row of wagon wheel light fixtures high above them, marching along the center beam from one end of the room to the other.

They continued to gaze about the large area. On their right, a stone fireplace with a raised hearth made from basketball-sized river rocks anchored one end of the living room. A sweeping set of stairs next to it, treads and railings crafted from aspen logs, climbed to the second floor.

Across the room in front of them, a two-story bank of windows framed a view of the western pass still piled with snow. Chairs and sofas covered in brown and white mottled cowhide were scattered throughout the space. To their left, a table, long enough to feed a dozen, took up most of the space. Beyond, a pair of swinging doors, obviously salvaged from an old saloon, hid a kitchen.

Spying breakfast laid out on the table, they hurried

over to one end of the table already set for four. Stacks of pancakes and platters of bacon, eggs, toast, and fresh grilled trout steamed next to pitchers of milk and juice. On the nearby sideboard, an earthy aroma rose from the coffee maker sputtering cheerfully as it brewed away.

Griffin reached for the trout even before his bottom hit the chair. "Guess these are mine," he crowed. "Seeing that you and Basil are Wind and Waters." After sliding all the fish onto a plate, he added half a dozen pancakes and began attacking the meal. "I hope Sukalli sticks around and cooks for us."

Sergei mumbled something around a mouthful of toast and bacon. They both looked up, their cheeks bulging, when the other two stepped inside.

As Basil made a beeline for the coffee, Sukalli walked over and sat down next to Griffin. "Do you still have that sketch you drew of the pendant Nicopolis was wearing?"

"I have it." Taking a seat next to Sergei, Basil handed it across the table to the Guardian. "Here it is."

As the other three watched, Sukalli smoothed the paper open on the table and studied the drawing. He looked up at the Mentor. "Dang."

"Is it what I think it is?" Basil asked.

Sukalli nodded. "I think so. I'll show it to Mayla just to make sure, but you were right to suggest this place. It is one of the few sanctuaries Command has been able to fortify with Might. Only a handful of us know of its location, so you three should be fairly safe here."

"Will it stop him? Even with..." Basil pointed at the

drawing.

"Hope so. Or at least, slow him down." Folding the paper, Sukalli tucked it in his pocket and rose. He nodded toward the swinging doors leading to the kitchen. "Now, the lodge is well-stocked, so you all should be fine to hunker down here for awhile." He tapped Griffin on the shoulder. "The stream out back is full of browns, rainbows, and even some cutthroat trout, pup. You might try some fishing. And I've let Dimitri know you're okay," he said to Sergei. "Basil, I'll be in touch later." With a nod, he took two steps and vanished with a soft *whoosh*.

"After we finish up, we'll unpack the Jeep and go exploring." Basil took another sip of coffee, then looked around the dirty table. "Griffin, you've earned first turn at cleanup duty."

"Why me?"

"Because you disobeyed me and sneaked out after I forbid you to go to Cas' party."

"Um, Basil?" Sergei held up a hand. "Actually, I'm as much to blame as Griffin. I was part of that decision, too. "With that, he stood up and began gathering plates. He glanced over at Griffin. "Dude—your mouth is hanging open. Close it before a fly gets in." Hands full, he disappeared into the kitchen.

* * *

Stepping into his assigned room, Griffin dropped his duffle on the comforter. He made a face when the bedsprings gave off a squeak. Dumping his book bag on the floor next to the small desk, complete with a lamp made from deer antlers, he pulled out his laptop and plugged it in, then walked around the bed to the window.

The U-shaped valley, crafted from the crawl of a glacier during the last ice age, spread out before him. To the west, the mountain range, with its pass flanked on either side by two peaks, gleamed in the midday sun. Snow still covered most of the higher elevations. A breeze ruffled the surface of the beaver pond. "It's like being inside a John Denver song." With a laugh, he headed out of the door and down the hall to Sergei's room.

"This must be some kind of dude ranch or a resort," he said to Sergei as he hovered in the doorway watching him unpack. "There's a bunch of empty bedrooms at the far end of the hallway."

"But a dude ranch without the horses. That would have been fun if they had some here."

"Wow—you know how to ride?"

"Yeah. Dimitri taught me. He used to make jokes about Cossacks and all that."

"He sounds like he was a cool Mentor."

Sergei reached around the desk and plugged in his own laptop before answering. "Yup. Of course, he is the only one I've had. Not counting those few weeks with Basil." He stood up, a question on his face. "Hey, I've been meaning to ask you something. About something Nicopolis said when—"

Griffin tensed. "I better go see if Basil wants me to do anything." He whirled around and hurried across the hall. The Mentor's door stood ajar. Without knocking, he pushed it open and slipped inside.

Basil looked up from his unpacking, then paused. "Anything amiss?"

"Just came to see if you needed any help."

Basil sighed. "Promise me you will never play poker. You are a terrible liar." He pulled out several shirts from the bag resting on the bed and folded them neatly before placing them in the dresser. "Are you and Sergei butting heads again?" he asked over a shoulder.

"Nah, not really."

"Then what?" As Griffin hesitated, Basil continued. "You might as well tell me. I'll pry it out of you sooner than later."

"He wants to know about something Nicopolis mentioned during the fight." Griffin sank down on the foot of the mattress.

Basil pushed the bag out of the way and joined him. Side by side, they stared down at the Navajo rug covering the wooden floor. "And what was it that Nicopolis mentioned?"

"About how he used to...you know." Griffin clenched his fists as he stared at the geometric pattern by the tips of his shoes. "How he used to hit me."

For a moment, they sat without speaking. Then Basil bumped his shoulder against Griffin's, an old gesture.

"You have no reason to feel shame for what he did to you, lad. You know that. It wasn't you or any weakness or lack of ability that made him treat you so horribly."

"I know. But I just don't want Sergei to know about all that. He already thinks I'm this pathetic Tiro who's got all these issues. I just know he'll use what happened with Nicopolis against me somehow. To make my life miserable."

"Really? Well, from what I observed these last few days, he's been treating you more like a younger brother than a rival. Complete with the ubiquitous teasing. But he also has been there when you've needed him. Like a brother would."

"What are you saying? I should spill my guts to him? Tell him my deepest fears? Have a male-to-male bonding moment?" Griffin glanced sideways at the Mentor. "Come on, Basil, we're guys. We don't share feelings. We punch each other in the stomach."

Basil laughed. "Why, of course. I had forgotten what it was like being sixteen and eighteen respectively."

"That's because you're over a thousand years old," Griffin pointed out, relieved to have changed the subject.

"And feeling every century." Basil's eyes twinkled. He held up a hand as Griffin started to rise. "Let me just say this. It is your decision whether or not to tell Sergei about your history with Nicopolis. But I do believe he would not treat the information, or you, lightly. Even though he can be a bit..." Basil's voice faltered as he searched for the correct term.

"Stuck up?" Griffin supplied. "Full of crap?

"Opinionated about certain issues," Basil said. "But he has proven himself a true Terrae Angeli."

For a minute, Griffin chewed on the inside of his cheek. "Yeah, maybe you're right. I'll think about it."

Basil clapped a hand on Griffin's knee. "That's all I can ask. Now, let's go explore the ranch. I want to get a feel for the layout before dark."

Heading down the hall, they collected Sergei from his room. All three walked downstairs and across the great room.

"Back door," Basil said, leading the way toward the kitchen. He pushed through the swinging doors, the younger angels on his heels. Passing through the large, well-equipped kitchen to the Dutch door, they stepped outside.

They found themselves on a wide porch. Three wooden steps dropped down to a path that wound through the grass and past a nearby storage shed built to mimic the lodge. Beyond, a meadow about half the size of a football field swept up to the edge of the pond.

"Why, this is perfect," Basil said, looking around. "Plenty of room to train and a pond to cool off in afterwards. Brilliant." He walked down the steps and headed west on the trail. The other two tagged along in single file.

"What kind of training?" Griffin asked as he followed on Basil's heels. He noticed that he now only had to take one and a half steps to keep up with the tall Mentor's stride instead of two. "I hope I grow just one more inch. I hate being stuck at five eleven."

Sergei snorted. "Five eleven? Wow—I didn't think

you were even *that* tall. Now, when I was your age, I was already at six."

"Are you talking about your height?" Griffin retorted. "Or your I.Q?"

"You know, you're pretty funny," Sergei replied. "Funny looking, that is."

Hiding a smile, Basil spoke. "In answer to your earlier question, I am going to train you two in specific defensive techniques since it has become necessary for you to protect yourselves. It will also help sharpen *my* skills, as I have not practiced these for quite some years."

"Like how many years?" Sergei asked.

Basil thought for a minute. "Why, the battle of Agincourt, I believe."

"Agincourt? What's—" Sergei started to ask when Griffin spoke up.

"It was a military victory by the English over the French during the Middle Ages. Shakespeare wrote a play about it called *Henry the Fifth*. It had that famous speech by King Henry. You know the one. 'We few. We happy few. We band of brothers. For he today that sheds his blood with me shall be my brother.' And so on and so on. My history teacher read it to us." He snorted in amusement when the Mentor stopped and bowed his head.

"Thank you, Almighty One," Basil prayed aloud, "for allowing me to live long enough to hear my Tiro quote Shakespeare. You may take me now. Amen."

After making a loop through the meadow, they walked over to the pond, its water glowing in shades of amber and green. At one end, the beaver dam created a wide, deep pool. A massive weathered log jutted out from the bank, its lower half wedged between two large boulders. The tip of the log was suspended several feet above the center of the pool.

"It's like a natural diving platform." Sergei climbed onto it and walked along its length. He peered down into the water. "Looks deep enough."

Griffin ambled over to the end of the log where it rested on the bank and pretended to study a tall pine nearby. Whistling a tune between his teeth, he nonchalantly stomped his foot at the base of the boulders cradling the fallen tree.

The ground humped and buckled beneath his foot. With a low groan, the boulders shifted from side to side, rolling the log between them like a pair of hands.

"Hey, knock it off!" Sergei swayed forward and back as he fought to keep his footing. Flailing his arms, he lurched sideways and tumbled off. Just before he hit the water, he vanished, ruffling the surface of the pond.

"Now, Griffin, was that really necessary?" Basil scolded. "You're just antagonizing him."

"Hey, it's not my fault he has no sense of balance," Griffin said with a grin. His smile faded when a breeze whispered through the pines behind him. *Oh, crap.* He spun around.

A blast of Wind punched him in the chest. His feet left the ground. Stunned, he soared backwards and landed in the water with an almighty splash, sending a geyser shooting up into the air.

Then, Griffin sank like a stone.

Chapter Sixteen

Ripples spread across the pond from Griffin's entrance. They lapped the bank with a gurgling sound, then stilled.

At that moment, Sergei materialized on the shore with a pleased expression. "Guess that'll teach you to..."

"Oh, bloody hell!"

With a curse, Basil bolted past him and dove into the water. Keeping his momentum going with strong kicks, he angled downward to the figure sinking into the murky depths. With a surge of Might, he shot downward, bubbles streaming out behind him like a torpedo. Reaching out, he snagged one of Griffin's arms. A quick flip, another mighty kick, and he shot back to the surface, one arm holding the struggling apprentice around the chest. A few moments later, their heads broke the surface. Almost immediately, Griffin began gasping and retching.

"What were you thinking?" Basil yelled at Sergei, swimming one-armed to the bank as he hauled the Tiro along. "He's an Earth and Fire, for heaven's sake." Slogging through the shallow water, he helped Griffin out of the water and eased him down on the grass. He patted his back while Griffin crouched on hands and knees, coughing up pond water. "Try to breathe normally, lad."

"I-I don't understand." Sergei edged over to them. "All I did was—"

"Earth and Fires are terrible swimmers," Basil snapped. "For obvious reasons, they have less buoyancy than do us Wind and Waters. So swimming is difficult for them at the best of times." They both looked down in relief when the Tiro groaned and staggered to his feet.

"I-I don't know who-who's worse," Griffin wheezed, pushing dripping hair out of his eyes. "You or Nicopolis."

"Um, sorry about that, dude. I didn't know. Really."

Griffin stared daggers at him. "Yeah. Right."

While Basil pointed a finger at his clothing in an attempt to blow dry them, Griffin pulled his tee shirt off and wrung it out. Slipping it back on, he took a deep breath and squeezed his eyes tight. Steam began rising from his drenched shirt and jeans. His face reddened. After a few minutes, he opened his eyes. "That's about as dry as I can get."

After a minute, Basil gave up as well. "I do not relish spending the rest of the day in damp garments. Time to head back."

They made their way across the meadow. Halfway to the lodge, a gust whipped past their ears, bowing the tall grasses over and sending bits of stalks and twigs swirling through the air. The Mentor halted. He frowned and glanced about.

"Hey, it's not me." Sergei raised both hands in protest.

"What's wrong, Basil?" Griffin edged closer.

Basil cocked his head as if listening. "Incoming," he said in a matter-of-fact voice, then stepped to one side.

Before Griffin could move, a figure materialized in mid-air and slammed into him. Together, they crashed to the ground in a tangle of arms and legs. A heavy pack whacked Griffin on the side of head. Blinded by a mass of dark red hair falling in his face, he struggled against the weight pinning him to the ground. An elbow dug into his shoulder, then a girl's face appeared above his. Her wide hazel eyes blinked down at him.

"Are you always this clumsy?" she asked. Without waiting for an answer, she rolled to her feet. A second figure materialized next to them.

"Vassar!" yelled a female voice. "How many times have I told you, Tiro—watch where you land. Especially when you're carrying a load."

"Yeah, yeah. I know. Sorry," Vassar said, not sounding sorry at all. "But, believe me, as fast as I was coming in, it could have been a lot worse."

Griffin looked up, ear ringing from the blow. A female, petite and somewhat older than Vassar, stood over him. Dressed entirely in black, an over-stuffed travel duffel dangled from her shoulder. Something about her seemed familiar.

Dropping the bag, she reached a hand down to Griffin. "You okay?" she asked as she heaved him upright.

Griffin's eyes widened at the strength in her grip. "Yes, ma'am. I'm good."

With a nod, she turned to Basil. Her chin-length black hair framed a pale, oval face. Dark eyes tilted at the corners when she smiled up at the tall Mentor.

"Ah, Basil, how are you?" She arched a delicate eyebrow in confusion. "And why are you wet?"

"Hello, Nan-ja." Basil ignored her question. "By the Light, what are you doing here?"

"Sukalli sent for us—there's been a new development." Nan-ja waved a hand in dismissal when Basil opened his mouth. "And yes, I know what's going on, and yes, I'll fill you in later, but right now, let's take care of introductions." Nan-ja pointed at the teen girl. "This one with the non-existent braking ability is Vassar. My Tiro."

Vassar nodded politely to Basil before looking over at Griffin. "Really, I *am* sorry about that. I had a spilt second to decide whether to crash into you or crash into Basil, so I—"

"That is *Mentor* Basil to you," Nan-ja scolded.

"—Mentor Basil," Vassar said without missing a beat. She began brushing dust and grass off her faded jeans. Her fitted hoodie was a shade of orange that clashed brutally with her hair. "Thanks for breaking my fall—I would have landed right on my butt." Vassar looked up in mock innocence when her Mentor gave a

133

growl. "What? *Butt* is not a bad word. I mean, everyone's got one." Vassar turned back to Griffin and Sergei. "You guys both got one, right? A butt? Or do you say *ass*? Some people say ass, but Nan-ja doesn't like me to—"

"Vassar!"

Vassar grinned in amusement at the tone in her Mentor's voice. She studied Griffin and Sergei for a moment before glancing about the valley.

Griffin found himself staring. *An Earth and Fire like me*, he thought, noting the fiery hair and amber-colored eyes. He blinked when Nan-ja spoke.

"Griffin," she said, holding out her hand. "We didn't get a chance to speak at Miss Weiss's funeral. I'm so sorry for your loss—I know what she meant to you and Basil."

"Thank you."

"And I understand you've had quite an eventful year."

"Yes, ma'am." He wiped his hand clean on his shirt before shaking hers.

Nan-ja chuckled. "You are *definitely* one of Basil's. And I understand congratulations are in order for *you*," she added, turning her attention on Sergei. "One of the youngest Tiros ever promoted to full Terrae Angeli status—I'm impressed."

Straightening to his full height, Sergei swelled out his chest and gave a graceful nod of his head.

"We seem to be doing introductions in reverse order," Basil said. "Gentlemen, this is Mentor Nan-ja, an old and dear friend of mine." He offered his arm to her.

"Shall we go inside, then? And, Griffin, bring Mentor Nan-ja's kit for her." He headed for the cabin, Nan-ja beside him; the top of her head only just reached his shoulder.

Griffin paused to pick up the duffel. He watched with a scowl when Vassar and Sergei fall in behind the Mentors. *I should have known he would take off with her and leave me to play pack mule.* He hoisted the bag higher and started after them.

As they neared the lodge, Vassar glanced back. "So you're the famous Griffin," she said, shifting her backpack to her other shoulder. "Nah, I got it," she added as Sergei offered to carry it.

"What do you mean—*famous?*" Griffin picked up the pace and fell in beside her. He noticed she was a few inches shorter than him.

"Why, you know," Sergei chimed in. "That whole born-again angel thing." He leaned closer to Vassar's. "Did you hear the nickname the other Tiros were calling him?"

"No, what?"

"'Lucy.' Short for Lucifer. You know—a *fallen* angel."

Face burning, Griffin shoved past them and sped up toward the back door. Sergei's laughter followed. He took the steps two at a time, the duffle bouncing against his back, and slipped into the kitchen.

Basil stood at the sink, filling a kettle with water while Nan-ja relaxed at the round, wooden table. "Fin, run her things upstairs to the first bedroom, please," he

135

said, fiddling with the knobs on the stove. "Oh, and by the way, could you give me a light?" He gestured toward one of the burners. "Gas stove, don't you know."

Carry the bag. Light the stove. Sheesh, why don't I just clean the entire freaking cabin while I'm at it, Griffin grumbled to himself. *After I cook dinner for everyone!* He flicked a finger against his thumb and shot a spark at the burner, igniting it. Pushing through the swinging doors with a double *thump-slap*, he stalked out of the kitchen.

A sudden need to talk with Katie gnawed at him like a tooth ache as he walked upstairs. After reaching the second floor, he dropped the bag off and headed down the hall to his room. Fishing the cell phone out of his pocket, he walked over to the window and stared out. *I sure hope I can get reception.* He held it up at eye level.

Water dribbled out of the phone in a brown stream.

"Oh, Fire." He sank down on the window bench with a groan. After shaking it, pressing every button, and even heating it up between his hands in a vain effort to dry it out, he gave up and tossed it on the bed. Leaning back against the glass, he closed his eyes.

"Is there anything else?" he asked the empty room, "that could go wrong in my life?"

"You know you're tempting fate by asking that question," said an amused voice.

Griffin opened his eyes.

Vassar leaned on one shoulder in the doorway, thumbs hooked in the pockets of her jeans. "Because the answer just might be yes."

"What do you want? To take up where Sergei left off?"

Vassar raised her eyebrows at his tone, then shrugged. "Basil sent me to get you. I guess we're having a meeting." Spinning on her heels, she left.

Scrubbing his face, Griffin sighed and pushed off the bench. He followed Vassar downstairs.

Several armchairs and a sofa had been herded closer to the fireplace, forming a semi-circle of cowhide-covered shapes. A fire already blazed away in the hearth; burning pine scented the room. Vassar took a seat on the sofa next to her Mentor, while Basil settled in one of the armchairs. Sergei sat on the raised hearth. As Griffin sank down in the other armchair nearest to Vassar, Nan-ja began.

"I have been asked by Sukalli to come and spend some time with *the guys*," she said with a twinkle in her almond shaped eyes. "To assist Basil in training you two in some advanced techniques as well as help keep an eye out for Nicopolis. And it will give Vassar a chance to work with other Tiros. A win-win for everyone."

"Nan-ja," Basil said, shifting in his seat. "Being around us is too dangerous. I do not want more Terrae Angeli placed in harm's way just because Nicopolis—"

"Naturally, Basil is thrilled with this decision," she said to the others, ignoring him.

"I am not! In fact, I told Sukalli distinctly that I refuse—"

"As you can see, he cannot wait to get started. We'll

begin first thing in the morning." She held up her hand when Basil opened his mouth to protest. "You might as well accept the inevitable, my friend. We are here to stay, at least for awhile."

"Awesome." Sergei grinned. "Team Angel has just gone co-ed."

Chapter Seventeen

Griffin's Journal: Saturday, May 28th

Finally got to call Katie late this afternoon. The reception sucked – we barely talked for five minutes when Basil's stupid phone cut out on me. Man, I miss her.

And for the record, Basil is totally wrong about Sergei.

Ser-jerk.

He's already acting like a *you-know-what* around Vassar. He went right back to being a jerk to me just to impress her. Hope they had a good laugh at his Lucy joke.

* * *

Closing the laptop, Griffin rubbed his eyes, then glanced over at the bed. *Might as well grab a nap before dinner.* He rose from the desk. Kicking his shoes off, he flopped down on the bed with a creak of springs. Folding his arms beneath his head, he closed his eyes against the final rays of the setting sun coming through the window.

"Hey."

Griffin slitted one eye.

Sergei stood in the half opened doorway. He pushed it wider and stepped inside. "Listen, about what happened earlier. Both at the pond and the whole Lucy thing—sorry about all that."

Griffin opened his other eye. "You are so full of crap, you know that? You just couldn't wait to make me look stupid."

Sergei's face reddened. "I'm trying to apologize."

"Yeah, whatever. Now get out of my room. Ser-jerk."

At that moment, Vassar appeared behind Sergei's shoulder. "What's going on?" Without waiting for a response, she edged inside, looking from one angry face to another. "Are you guys fighting?"

"Nah." Sergei curled his lip. "He's just being an infant. As usual. He can't take a joke about anything."

With a growl, Griffin rolled off the bed. Stalking over to Sergei, he crowded him chest to chest. "The only joke around here is *you*. You're supposed to be this golden boy Terrae Angelus, but when push came to shove, Nicopolis knocked you out cold. If I hadn't saved your neck, you'd be dead right now!" All the fear and frustration from the last twenty-four hours spilled into his gut like a red tide. Without warning, he shoved Sergei backwards against the wall. Hard.

"Um...guys?" Vassar began.

Sergei staggered a step before catching his balance. He narrowed his eyes. "You really want a piece of *me*?" he said softly.

140

"Like I said before, you don't got the juice." Griffin shoved Sergei again.

With twin snarls, they lunged for each other.

* * *

Basil burst through the swinging doors from the kitchen, Nan-ja on his heels. A crash, followed by harsh cries and repeated thumping sounds, echoed down the stairs. Vassar's voice rose in frustration.

"Nicopolis?" Nan-ja asked as the Mentors raced across the great room toward the steps.

"We should be so lucky," Basil replied, his face dark with annoyance.

Before they could reach the first tread, a pair of figures came tumbling down the stairs, arms and legs flailing. Curses filled the air. The two Mentors jumped out of the way.

"At least they're not using their Elements against each other," Nan-ja shouted over the fray.

"Not yet." Basil stepped closer. Reaching down, he snagged both of them by the back of their shirts and yanked them apart. They stood panting, their eyes boring into each other.

Sergei sported a split lip. Blood smeared his chin like he was a character in a bad vampire movie. A bruise high on one cheekbone was already turning blue.

Right eye swelling shut, Griffin swiped at a bloody nose. His torn tee shirt hung from one shoulder.

Vassar appeared behind them, sauntering down the

steps. "If that was a demonstration of how well they can fight, we're all are *so* screwed."

"Vas, that's enough," Nan-ja said. "This is no time for one of your comments."

Arms folded across his chest, Basil fixed an ice-blue gaze on Griffin and Sergei. Jaw muscles danced as he stared at them.

He's counting to a hundred, Griffin thought. *I know that expression.* He pulled up the hem of his shirt and dapped at his still dripping nose.

"Nice abs," Vassar smiled in Griffin's direction as she brushed past to join the Mentors. Griffin blushed and hurriedly tugged the tee back down.

Nan-ja snagged her Tiro's arm. "Let's go finish preparing dinner."

"Ah, come on, Nan, you know I don't do the whole kitchen scene. I'm a warrior, not a chef."

"Time to expand your skill set. Move it."

They left the room. Basil waited until the kitchen doors stopped swinging before he began.

"This behavior ceases. Now," he said, voice glacial. He held up a hand as they both started protesting. "Sergei, I expected more from you. I expected behavior befitting a full-fledged Terrae Angelus. But you've not only let *me* down, your actions reflect badly on Dimitri and *his* training."

Sergei blushed. He began to speak, then gave up and nodded.

"And you, Tiro." Basil turned toward him.

Griffin swallowed. *Here it comes.*

"There are now *three* Terrae Angeli putting their lives on the line to keep you alive," Basil continued. "Not including the efforts being put forth by Sukalli and Mayla, as well as Flight Command. Yet, you waste time and energy engaged in petty squabbling and testosterone-induced brawling." His eyes bore into Griffin's. "At the very time I need you focused and ready to face these worsening days. And while I would willingly lay down my life for you, please do not make it necessary for me to do so by your cavalier behavior. Do you understand?"

Remorse cut like a knife through Griffin. "Yes, sir," he whispered. Ashamed to meet his Mentor's eyes, he shifted his gaze to Basil's elbow.

"Go upstairs, both of you. Fix whatever needs fixed. Be it furniture or each other. Then I want you down here acting civilized." Without another word, he spun around and marched to the front door. It slammed shut behind him with a boom.

Griffin looked at Sergei. Sergei stared back. They both let out a long breath at the same time.

Sergei licked at the blood on his lip. "He's good."

"Oh, yeah. He's the master of the guilt trip lecture." Griffin paused, certain he would be slapped down again. He plowed on anyway. "Listen, Sergei, we don't have to *like* each other. But we better start dealing with the fact that we're stuck here with each other. Agreed?"

"Yeah, I guess." Sergei glanced toward the kitchen and the sound of Vassar complaining to Nan-ja about antiquated gender roles. A cocky grin lit up his battered face. "Could be worse. And since you've got Katie already, hands off of Vassar."

Griffin's eyebrows shot up. "Vassar doesn't strike me as a girl you can call *first dibs* on."

"Right. Like you're such an expert on them."

"Just saying."

Still arguing, they made their way back up the stairs.

Chapter Eighteen

Basil stepped to the edge of the porch and stood there, looking down the entrance road as it disappeared into the aspens. Frustration tightened his face. After a moment, he marched down the steps and followed a trail around the corner of the lodge.

"Hey," called a voice as he reached the back of the building. "Where are *you* headed?"

"For a walk, Nan-ja, before I wring both their necks." He kept going, eyes fixed on the distance pond. A rustle. The other Mentor appeared next to him.

"Fine. I'll go with you."

Skirting the pond, they strolled through the meadow and into the woods on the far side. The evening sky darkened as clouds began boiling over the pass, pushed by the prevailing winds from the west. A hint of rain cooled the air.

After a half-hour hike in silence, Basil glanced out of the corner of his eye. "So. Are you going to fill me in, Nan-ja?"

"While I *am* here to do some training with those two, as well as with Vassar," she said as they worked their way through the thick pines. "I am also here at Sukalli's request. He wanted you to have another layer of protection after Sergei's failure at the last encounter—he contacted me less than an hour after he left here this morning."

"Why?" Basil pulled her to a stop to face him. "What has happened?"

"Command is hearing rumors that Nicopolis may have recruited some of his old cronies to aid in this vendetta."

"Does Sukalli know who they might be?"

"He thinks they may be some of the more radical traditionalists. The same ones who have complained over the years that our choices and lifestyles are too much like mortals. And, worse, that we're losing our angelic essence. They've actually formed an order—they call themselves the *Lightbringers*."

"Now that's a bit of propaganda. What's their goal?"

"You're not going to believe this, but they think Wind and Water are the only *true* Terrae Angeli. They want to eradicate every Earth and Fire as well as any Wind and Waters who does not measure up to their twisted standards. According to Sukalli, they call it a *purification* of our kind."

"Incredible." Basil shook his head. "Why, it's like the Nazis and their pogroms against the Jews. And most likely, Nicopolis has convinced them to begin with Griffin as an example."

"Well, if history tells us anything, it's that every radical group needs a scapegoat."

Basil tilted his head back and looked up through the tree tops at the growing storm. "What are we becoming, Nan-ja?"

"I don't know, my friend. But, in the meantime, Command thought you could use a little help. They would have sent more Terrae Angeli, but we're spread so thin right now that Vassar and I were all that could be spared." Nan-ja shook her head. "Poor Griffin. Talk about walking around with a target on his back."

"Not only him. You and Vassar and Sergei, and even the Guardians Mayla and Sukalli, are now just as vulnerable."

"Heck, Vass and I can take care of ourselves. And Sukalli is an angelic host of one."

"And Mayla?" Basil's lips twitched with amusement when Nan-ja made a face.

"Oh, I'm sure *she* would simply negotiate her way out of any confrontation—she wouldn't want to chip a nail."

"Jealousy does not become you."

"Right. Like I'm jealous of someone who never wears anything, but a dress."

"It's a sari."

"Whatever. Face it, Basil, your girlfriend is a total girly-girl."

His face reddened. "First of all, Mayla is not my *girlfriend* nor was she ever. We are simply old friends. Just as you and I are. Secondly," he continued, voice rising as he spoke. "I thought we were discussing Griffin, not my personal life!"

Nan-ja laughed and held up her hands in surrender. "All right, all right, calm down. I'll stop teasing you. For now."

"Thank you."

Thunder rumbled overhead. As the first drops fell, Nan-ja took Basil's arm. They started back. "Speaking of Griffin. After all he's been through in his life, I'm surprised he's holding up as well as he appears to be."

"Oh, Fin is strong in many ways. More than he knows."

"You're very fond of him, aren't you?"

"I am." Basil sighed. "As Mentors, we are not to have favorites, but..." He let the rest of the sentence fade.

"I understand." Nan-ja squeezed his arm. "He's more like a son to you than an apprentice."

Basil nodded. "And Griffin will make a remarkable Terrae Angelus when his time comes."

"Then we'll just have to keep him alive until then."

"Amen to that."

* * *

Opening the front door, Basil stepped aside, allowing Nan-ja to enter first; their clothes and hair damp from the rain. They both froze in astonishment at the scene before them,

Fire snapped and crackled in the fireplace, hissing when a stray drop of rain made its way down the chimney. At the opposite end of the room, the dining room table was already set for six. On the table, baskets of hot wheat rolls sat steaming on either side of an assortment of cheeses. Fat candles graced the center of the table; their flickering flames added a cozy warmth to the atmosphere.

As the Mentors stood awestruck, the swinging doors flapped open.

Vassar appeared first, carrying a large bowl filled with salad greens and tomatoes. Sergei came next, the cut on his lower lip still fresh. He held a pitcher of iced tea in one hand and a jug of water in the other. Close behind, Griffin edged through backwards with a sizzling platter, one side loaded with steaks, the other with grilled trout. When he turned around, his swollen eye made him appear to be winking.

"Before you get the wrong idea," Sergei said as Griffin put the platter on one end of the table. "*I* prepared the steaks and trout."

"Hey, I heated up the rolls," Vassar pointed out.

"Yeah, after you lit one of the baskets on fire." Sergei placed the jugs on the nearby sideboard. "And just for the record—wicker burns."

"It appears we've entered the wrong lodge," Basil said to Nan-ja.

She nodded absently as she eyed the table. "Pinch me. I must be dreaming."

At that moment, the front door blew open behind them. Sukalli stomped in, leather jacket beaded with moisture. He shrugged out of it and hung it on a rack of antlers nailed to the wall. "Howdy all. Glad to see everyone is still in one piece." Joining the Mentors, he studied Griffin and Sergei. "Well, sort of." And before Basil could question him, he pointed his chin at the table. "My news can wait. Let's eat first."

"I like an angel that's got his priorities straight." Sergei waved a hand toward the table.

Everyone scurried to claim a seat. Dishes and platters and baskets were passed back and forth across the table. Sukalli, Nan-ja, Vassar, and Griffin divvied up the trout while Basil and Sergei piled the steaks on their plates. The sound of eating and compliments about the food filled the room.

After half an hour of feasting, Sukalli pushed his plate aside. "Good eatin', you three. My thanks." He glanced around the table. "And, since it seems everyone is done, I guess I'll get down to business." Suddenly grim-faced, he looked at Basil. "Your suspicions were dead on, brother. Nicopolis appears to have found an *arba'a*."

"Bloody hell—I was afraid of that." Tossing his napkin down on the table, Basil sat back. "How did Nicopolis come to be in possession of it? I thought Mayla had the only *arba'a* still in existence?"

"Our best guess is that he found it during his mission in the Middle East," Sukalli said. "According to our ancient records, the city of Damascus was the last know location of the other ones."

"What an *arba'a* do?" asked Griffin. "Who made them?"

"Who created them, we don't know. They've been a part of our kind's history since the beginning. The *arba'a* is a mighty powerful device—it magnifies the wearer's powers." Sukalli hesitated, then continued. "One of its uses is to turn a Terrae Angelus mortal."

The blood drained from Griffin's face. "Is that what Nicopolis was going to do to Sergei and me?"

"Maybe. But more likely, he was going to use it to destroy you." Sukalli gazed across the table at Griffin, his bronze face sad. "As you know from first-hand experience, there is a fine line between becoming mortal and dying. Used a certain way, the *arba'a* can kill."

"So why didn't it work?"

Sukalli shrugged. "Mayla explained that it takes time, concentration, and practice to use the *arba'a*. Lucky for us, Nicopolis was probably distracted, and in a hurry due to Griffin's recovery and subsequent attack, when he tried it on Sergei. But you can be sure he'll do better next time. He's a fast learner."

"What happens if an *arba'a* is used against a human?" Nan-ja asked.

"Funny thing—it has no effect on mortals. In fact, Mayla said that if a Terrae Angelus tries to use it to harm a person, the power rebounds off the mortal and destroys the angel who was stupid enough to try."

"Or evil enough," Griffin said.

"What does *arba'a* mean?" Vassar asked.

"It means *four* in Arabic. An allusion to our Elements, you might say."

"Earth and Fire," murmured Griffin and Vassar in unison.

"Wind and Water," added Sergei.

"This may sound morbid, and my apologies to you, Tiro, but why wouldn't Nicopolis just simply kill Griffin outright?" Nan-ja asked. "By using Might or one of his Elements or even his bare hands? He's certainly has the ability."

"Perhaps a need for a dramatic gesture?" Basil said. "Or some other reason? It's hard to explain his perverse way of thinking." He shrugged and looked at Sukalli. "By the way, Nan-ja informed me of the latest developments. Do you know precise numbers yet or who is involved?"

"What's do you mean, *latest development?*" Sergei asked. "Is there something we should know?"

"Nicopolis is not only packing an *arba'a*," Sukalli said, "but it looks like he might be rounding up a posse to help him. Heaven help us if he was able to find more *arba'as.*"

Vassar leaned closer to Griffin. "What's with all the cowboy idioms?" she whispered. "I feel like an extra in a John Wayne movie." Griffin started to speak, then stopped when Nan-ja elaborated.

"There's a rumor going around that Nicopolis has persuaded or coerced others to join him. Others who have become disgruntled with the Terrae Angeli in general."

At the younger angels' surprised expressions, Basil explained. "There are those among us who believe we

152

have become too *down to earth* lately, both in our life-styles and in our philosophies. They feel we should be more aloof. More detached. More *angelic*. And their numbers are growing."

"Like-like how detached?" Griffin asked, the dinner settling in his stomach like a cannon ball.

"If they had their way, lad, then certainly your relationship with Katie would be prohibited. Even casual acquaintances would be discouraged. They've even suggested discontinuing the practice of staffing the Foundation with mortals. But there is even a more sinister side to them. It's about Earth and Fire angels—"

At that moment, lightning from the growing storm exploded outside in a neon flash. The front door crashed open. A gust of wind, scented with rain, snuffed out the candles and sent napkins flying off the table like startled pigeons.

Nearest to the door, Griffin leaped to his feet. Basil pushed him back down. "Stay put." He rose and slipped across the room, Sukalli and Nan-ja on his heels. Sergei stepped around the table and took up a position in front of Griffin.

Basil paused in the open doorway. He nodded when Sukalli muttered something, then stepped outside, followed by the other two. Thunder growled as they disappeared.

"You must be some special Tiro to have this much angel power guarding your butt." Vassar stood up and began re-lighting the candles with a flaming fingertip.

Griffin tightened his lips. Guilt and embarrassment arm-wrestled for attention inside of him. "It's not like I asked them to do it."

"And yet, here we all are—babysitting," Sergei said over his shoulder, eyes fixed on the doorway. All three tensed at the sound of a hollow thump on the porch.

A moment later, Basil stepped inside. He shook his head, scattering water droplets. "All clear. Sukalli and Nan-ja are reconnoitering, just to be sure."

"Do you want me to go help them?" Sergei asked.

"No need." Sukalli and Nan-ja entered.

Stopping to close and lock the door behind her, Nan-ja shrugged. "Not that a lock would stop them," she said. "And it could be the wind simply blew it open."

Sukalli grabbed his jacket from the coat hook. "Well, I better hit the trail. Now that we have two teams out of rotation, we're stretched as thin as—"

"—a cheap saloon's whiskey," suggested Sergei.

"—a Puritan's pancake," added Vassar.

"—Nicopolis' hair," finished Griffin.

Chapter Nineteen

Basil's Journal: Sunday, May 29th

Nan-ja and I talked for quite some time last night after the others (nay I say the children?) had gone to bed. We both agree there are grim days ahead. Not just for us personally, but for all the Terrae Angeli. Are we witnessing the beginning of a new, radical movement? One that may drive us asunder in ways we cannot predict?

As a great man once said: 'A house divided against itself cannot stand.'

Griffin's Journal: Sunday, May 29th

Yesterday was the freaking weirdest day of my life! I started to write it all down, but then deleted it. It was beginning to sound like those Mortal Devices books (or whatever they're called) Katie reads. Nephilim. Right. Like *those* guys are real.

* * *

Griffin pressed the save button and powered down the computer. Turning from the desk, he gazed out the window, watching as the dawn brightened the western mountains, the snow on their tips like pink ice cream.

Raking his fingers through hair still damp from a shower, he rose and headed out. Mindful of the early hour, he crept along the hall, shaking his head at the sound of clacking computer keys coming behind Basil's closed door. *Does the guy ever sleep?*

He made his way down the stairs, the aroma of brewing coffee pulling him by the nose. Pushing through the swinging doors into the kitchen, he paused when he spied Vassar already seated at the table, a steaming mug in one hand.

"It must an Earth and Fire thing," she said, raising her cup in greeting. Her braided hair draped like a red rope over one shoulder.

"What, drinking coffee?"

"Nope—being early risers. Heck, Nan-ja has been outside for an hour, prepping that large meadow for today's training session."

"What kind of training?"

"I think she wants to see what you guys can do." Vassar's amber eyes danced. "You better eat your Wheaties."

Griffin poured himself a mug of coffee, walked over to the back door, and opened it. Cool air, tangy from wet pines, flowed over him. He stepped outside.

Cupping the mug in his hands, he watched as Nan-ja carried a board nearly as tall as herself to the far end of the meadow. Setting it down on its end, she jammed it into the ground and wiggled it into place. Two other boards, similar in length, stood at attention nearby. She pulled a marker out of a pocket and began drawing bull's eyes on the three makeshift targets.

Scanning the area, Griffin noticed other items: wooden crates, an old wheelbarrow, a couple of paint cans, and even a selection of tools such as shovels and rakes. He frowned at the coils of rope scattered here and there.

"What's with the ropes?" he asked over his shoulder.

Vassar joined him, coffee in hand. "I don't know. But Nan's always thinking up crazy things for training—but, I've learned a lot from her." She waved a hand to catch the Mentor's attention, then pointed to her cup. Nan-ja gave a nod and began making her way across the meadow toward them. Her shoes left twin streaks in the rain-soaked grass.

Raising his face to sky, Griffin inhaled. "This place is awesome. I wish we were here just for fun or a vacation."

"You mean, being on the run from a lunatic who wants to murder you isn't your idea of fun? What kind of Tiro are you?" Vassar glanced over at him. "By the way, your eye looks almost normal."

Griffin fingered it gingerly. "Good. This is my second black eye in a week. Must be a record for me. I'm just glad Katie's not here to see it."

"Is she your girlfriend?"

"Yeah, Katie Heflin. She lives across the street from Basil and me."

"She's mortal, right?" As Griffin's nod, Vassar continued. "And Basil lets you date a human? Do her folks know about you guys."

"Yup. And they're totally cool with it. So's Basil."

Vassar looked down into her coffee. "What's she like?"

"Wicked smart, really pretty, and a great cross country runner."

"She's sounds perfect."

Griffin nodded in agreement. "So, what about you?" he asked as he took another sip.

"Oh, I'm perfect, too."

Coffee spewed from Griffin's mouth. Swiping his chin with the back of a hand, he laughed. "Funny. No, I meant, do you have a boyfriend?"

Vassar shook her head. "Naw—no time." She stepped over to the edge of the porch as Nan-ja walked up. "Morning, Nan."

"Morning, Vass." The Mentor trotted up the stairs and paused to tug the end of the apprentice's braid. "I like your hair that way." She smiled over at Griffin. "And good morning to you, Griffin. Or do you go by Fin?"

"I go by Griffin. Fin is just a nickname Basil calls me." He walked over to the cupboard and pulled out another cup. "Can I get you some coffee, Mentor Nan-ja?"

Nan-ja took a seat at the table along with Vassar. "Coffee would be lovely, thank you. Cream only. And drop the Mentor stuff. Basil's not around, so you don't need to act like a proper English gentleman."

The swinging doors creaked open. Basil stepped through. "Actually, he does." He wore a faded sweatshirt over his jeans. "Good morning all," he said, joining Nan-ja and Vassar. He smiled in gratitude when Griffin brought mugs of coffee for both Mentors. After serving them, he pulled out a chair and sat down.

"So, Nan-ja," Basil said after taking a drink. "What is on the agenda for today?"

"I'm going to have Sergei and Griffin show me what they can do with their Elements. That way, I'll know where to start with them." She cocked an eye at Vassar. "In some ways, all this is good timing as I've wanted to accelerate Vassar's training now that she's a Senior Tiro."

"When was your Proelium?" Griffin asked Vassar.

"This past winter solstice."

"Same as mine."

"And I barely made it outside the circle in time." She made a face at the memory. "How was yours? Did you..." Her voice trailed off when Nan-ja cleared her throat in warning. Vassar blushed. "Oh, sorry."

Griffin shrugged. "It's okay. Heck, everyone knows what happened with *my* Proelium." He held the mug between his palms, watching as the coffee began bubbling. "So I guess that makes us about the same age?"

"Yeah, sixteen."

At that moment, Sergei staggered half awake through the swinging doors. "Coffee," he mumbled as he made a beeline for the coffee machine.

The corner of Griffin's mouth quirked. "Just drank it all. You really should have gotten up earlier." He lifted the cup to his lips.

Without breaking stride, Sergei bumped the back of Griffin's chair with a hip as he passed by. The mug banged against Griffin's teeth and sloshed most of the liquid down his shirt. With a growl, he shoved his chair back, sending Sergei stumbling into Vassar.

"Hey!" She snatched her own mug out of harm's way. "Watch it!"

"Griffin!" Basil clamped an iron hand on the apprentice's arm.

"But he—"

"Sergei, was that necessary?" The Mentor asked.

"Absolutely."

Basil ground his teeth in frustration and looked over at Nan-ja. "Will the training you have planned for us be physically demanding?"

"Mostly likely."

"So grueling that these two will be exhausted by each day's end?"

Nan-ja's eyes twinkled. "Why, yes, it will. Incredibly grueling, especially with what I have in mind."

"Excellent. Then you may begin with Griffin here. Drive him hard."

Griffin yanked free of Basil's grasp. "Why are you picking on *me*? Sergei started it." Before Basil could answer, he added something under his breath. Almost the instant it left his mouth, he cringed. *Uh-oh.*

"Outside, Tiro," Basil said in a cold undertone. "Now."

Red-faced, Griffin followed the Mentor out the back door and closed it behind him. "Look, it just slipped out.

Sorry I said—" He yelped when Basil grabbed his ear between thumb and forefinger in a pinching grip. "Aw, man, not the ear thing!"

"Not only did I catch that extremely offensive remark you just made, but once again, you and Sergei cannot wait to have a go at one another. While I do not have *direct* authority over him, I do over you." He pinched harder, giving the ear a twist for good measure. "And do you know what that means?"

Griffin hunched his shoulders, eyes watering. "You're going to take it out on me when he's the one being a jerk?"

"Exactly."

"But that's not fair. Ow!"

"Alas, life is terribly cruel that way. Injustice is a burden we all must bear from time to time." Basil released him. Griffin rubbed his ear. "If you wish to avoid this embarrassing and rather painful occasion again, I suggest you make better choices with both your comments and your actions. I am not having another day like yesterday. Do I make myself clear?"

Griffin's mouth worked as he struggled *not* to say what he wanted to say. He huffed out a breath through his nose.

"I'm waiting, Tiro."

"Okay."

"Okay what?"

"You made yourself clear. *Sir*," he added, barely stopping himself from rolling his eyes. He started to go back inside when Basil snagged his elbow.

"And I want you to listen closely to Nan-ja and learn everything you can. Although the circumstance may be less than desirable, I am grateful for this opportunity for you to train under a Mentor of her caliber."

"I'll try. So, is she better than you?"

"In some arenas, yes."

"Wow. I bet *that* hurt to admit it."

Basil smiled. "Cheeky brat."

"Always." He grinned back, grateful his Mentor was able to move past their rare skirmishes so quickly. Looking down at his shoes, he added. "Listen. I'm sorry I was rude."

Basil leaned back against the railing with an amused expression. "I may regret informing you of this, but I find your episodes of teenage rebellion quite heartwarming. And a great relief." He chuckled when Griffin's jaw dropped. "Don't you understand, Fin? Three years ago, you would flinch if I so much as *sneezed*. Now look at you. Why, you grumble and butt heads with me and sulk about the house with the best of them. Fearless."

Stunned by his Mentor's disclosure, Griffin stood frozen. "I, um..." He cleared his throat. "I was never really *afraid* of you, you know. Not like I was of Nicopolis."

"For that, I am grateful."

Me, too, Griffin thought. *More than you'll ever know.*

Straightening, Basil shooed him toward the door. "We best finish breakfast. If I know Nan-ja, you've a long day ahead of you."

Chapter Twenty

Panting, Griffin stumbled to a halt. He clasped his hands on the top of his head. The late morning sun baked him as he walked around the meadow, chest heaving. Nearby, Nan-ja tapped a foot while she waited for him to catch his breath. On the other side of the field, Basil was instructing Vassar and Sergei.

This altitude is killing me, Griffin thought, blinking the sweat out of his eyes. *I wouldn't have guessed four thousand more feet in elevation would make that much of a difference.* He grimaced when Nan-ja gestured at him.

"You're not finished." she called. "I said ten and I meant ten."

With a groan, Griffin dropped his arms. "And I thought Basil could be a hard ass about training," he muttered.

He flexed his hands a few times, then snapped them open. Fire blasted from his fingertips like miniature flame throwers. With a spinning motion, he leaped into the air. The flames from his fingers spiraled around him, charring the grasses in a perfect circle. Six other rings of black ash, about five yards in diameter, marked earlier efforts. He landed in the center of the latest one and looked over at Nan-ja.

She shook her head. "Nope. You're still not doing it during *real* flight. You're just jumping up and down."

"But I can't handle my Elements while I'm flying! I never could. I mean, even Basil's not that good at it." *Although I did manage it that one time when I lit the cuff of his pant leg on fire.* He dragged a hand across his face, smearing it with sweat and ash. "Isn't it time for lunch yet?"

Nan-ja ignored him. "I know this is hard, Griffin, and I don't expect you to master it right away. If it will make you feel any better, Vassar still can't do it either, and she's been training with me her whole life. In fact, most Terrae Angeli don't even bother to push themselves to this level since it is incredibly difficult to harness and control our Elements during flight." She thought for a moment. "Try igniting your Fire *after* you begin flying. See if that works for you. *Wakarimasu ka?*"

"What's that mean?"

"It means *do you understand* in Japanese. The correct response would be *hai.* Which means 'yes.'"

Griffin nodded. "*Hai.*" He licked dry lips as he stepped back a few feet. Sucking in a deep breath, he bent his knees, then threw himself into the air.

Silver light enveloped him like a mist with the sun shining through it. Colors became muted. Sound softened. As he soared over the meadow, he glanced down between his feet at the pond, a blue bowl on a green tablecloth. *I wonder why humans think angels fly through the air horizontally as if they were swimming. Talk about landing in a belly flop.* He shook his head at the image and focused on the task. He spread his arms slightly away from his body, fingers spread and hands pointing toward the ground. "As they say in the movie, *flame on!*" he shouted. With a roar, Fire erupted from his fingertips.

Griffin's head snapped back. Rocketing straight up, the wind screamed in his ears as the velocity increased with every second.

"Holy crap!" He gasped in alarm as the valley shrunk beneath his feet. Glancing through tearing eyes, he saw the peaks of the western mountains draw even with him. Without thinking, he clenched his fists and pulled out of flight.

For a split second, he hung there. A voice from the past spoke in his head.

You must never come to a complete halt in mid-flight, Tiro, for it is almost impossible to re-launch ourselves. Remember, we are not celestial angels, we are earth *angels. We require a solid surface to push against. So, be mindful of your actions whilst flying.*

What happens if I accidentally stop in mid-air, Mentor?

What do you think?

Griffin fell.

Gravity and wind pressure twisted him around. The ground filled his vision as he rushed back toward it. He found himself tumbling head over heels. Flailing his arms, he tried to grab hold of anything. He heard a cry;

it took a moment for him to recognize his own voice. Squeezing his eyes shut, he continued to plummet from the sky.

Something solid, yet soft thumped into him, like being hit with a pillow. He felt himself slowing as if the air around him had grown *thicker* somehow. A giant, invisible hand stopped his out-of-control tumble and pulled him around so that he was falling backside first, but not as fast. Opening his eyes, he craned his head around and looked down.

Below him, the Mentors stood side by side near the pond, their arms held high and their hands pointed toward him. A tiny corner of Griffin's mind noticed the strain on both their faces. Basil shouted something at Nan-ja who gave a nod. They swung their arms in a synchronized motion. Griffin felt a tug along his entire body. He found his trajectory veering toward one side of the meadow.

Toward the pond.

Coming in at a flattened angle, Griffin steeled himself. *Fire, I hope this works.* With a gasp, he hit the surface of the water, then skipped along it three times like a pebble before stopping. Stunned by the impact, he sank downward into the murky depths until he came to rest in the mud at the bottom of the pond.

For a moment, he watched the sunlight shimmer and dance on the surface above him. He felt himself sinking further into the muck as if the Earth was welcoming him home.

On the shore, Basil dropped his arms and sank to the ground, chest heaving. Nearby, Nan-ja sat slumped over; Vassar squatting beside her with a worried expression. Basil looked up at the sound of running feet.

Sergei sprinted past. He dove off the bank, speared the water with nary a ripple, and disappeared. After a long minute, his head broke the surface. Spitting out a mouthful, he locked eyes with Basil.

"I can't find him!"

Lurching to his feet, Basil staggered toward the water. He stumbled once, almost going down, then flung himself into the pond with a clumsy splash. He followed Sergei back under the surface.

It was like swimming through concrete. Arms and legs refused to work. Before the Mentor could gather his strength, a hand grabbed the front of his shirt and yanked him upward. His head broke the surface, followed by Sergei's.

Basil struggled, trying to pull free. "Release me this instant," he demanded hoarsely.

"No way. Not after over-extending yourself like that," Sergei growled back, dragging him over to the shore. "Nan-ja, come get this stubborn-ass Mentor before he drowns himself. Vassar, you and I are going back down. I need an Earth and Fire to locate Griffin—I think he's buried in the mud at the bottom."

Basil started to argue, every fiber in his body screaming at him to leap back into the water. Then, his knees gave out. He looked up and locked eyes with the younger angel. "Hurry."

Sergei nodded. "Vassar—you're with me."

After kicking off her shoes, Vassar waded past him until the water was up to her neck. Sucking in a breath, she ducked down. Sergei dived in after her. As Basil watched them disappear, Nan-ja walked over on wobbly legs and joined him.

The Mentors waited, eyes fixed on the pond. Ripples ran up onto the shore before fading away. For another minute, they sat there. Then, with a rumble of frustration, Basil gathered his feet under him and prepared to rise.

"Oh, no, you don't." Nan-ja clamped a hand on his arm and tugged him back down. "Sergei has the right idea. He and Vassar will find him."

Basil clenched his jaw, worry and exhaustion twisting the muscles in back and shoulders. He stiffened at the sight of movement in the shadowy depths, then slumped with relief when one head, followed by two more, broke the surface with a splash a moment later. "Thank God," he breathed and stood up. Holding out a hand, he helped Nan-ja to her feet.

Scarcely able to keep her nose above water, Vassar struggled as she dogpaddled toward them. Her braid undulated behind her like a water snake. Sloshing up onto the bank, she bent over, hands on knees, gasping for air.

Nan-ja stepped over. "That's my girl," she said, patting her Tiro's back.

Behind them in the pond, Sergei swam one-handed

as he dragged an unconscious Griffin along. He stood up when he reached the shallows and began hauling his burden closer to land. Basil waded out to meet them.

"I've got him." Basil grabbed Griffin under the arms and pulled him onto the grassy bank. The Tiro's head flopped back, eyes closed and mouth slack. Wet mud clung to his clothes and face. Basil knelt beside him. "Fin? Can you hear me?" He tapped Griffin's cheek, then turned him onto his side. With an open hand, he slapped him a few times between the shoulder blades.

Griffin's body jerked. He gave a violent heave. Brownish water gushed from his mouth. His hands and legs twitched spasmodically while he retched and wheezed and retched again.

Relief softened Basil's features. He started to wipe the mud from Griffin's face, then paused at the faint whisper. "I'm sorry—what did you say?" He leaned closer.

"Dead?" Griffin rasped again.

Basil chuckled. "No, lad, you're not dead."

"Sure?"

"Quite certain."

"How is he?" Nan-ja stepped closer, Vassar and Sergei beside her.

"Half drowned, but, otherwise, fine," Basil said, helping Griffin roll over onto his back. He smiled when the Tiro peered at him through slitted eyes.

"I'm really, really beginning to hate that stupid pond," he croaked.

"Then stop falling in it," Sergei said. "Or do we need to put up a safety gate?"

"Oh, give it a rest, Sergei," Vassar said. "He almost died, you know."

"Yeah, but he didn't, thanks to me. He should be kissing my feet in gratitude right now."

Griffin wobbled as he sat up and spat mud out of his mouth. "If I kiss anyone," he said hoarsely, "it'll be Vassar. She's the one who dug me out."

"Ewww—that would be like kissing my brother."

The Mentors exchanged glances and chuckled. Then, Basil hauled Griffin upright. "All right, now?" At Griffin's nod, they began walking slowly back to the lodge. Sergei fell into step behind them. Nan-ja and Vassar followed, their arms linked together in mutual support. Reaching the lodge, the Mentors sent the Tiros to change into dry clothes.

Reaching his room, Griffin shut the door, then peeled off his filthy clothes. Leaving them in a pile on the bathroom floor, he showered and dressed. As he scrounged around in his duffle bag for dry shoes, someone knocked on the door. "It's open."

Sergei stuck his head inside. "Lunch is ready."

"Okay. Hey, wait a sec." Griffin walked over. "Uh, thanks. Basil told me what you did. You and Vassar."

"Just doing my job keeping you alive."

"Yeah, sorry about that."

Sergei braced a hand on the door jam. "Sorry about what?"

"You having to risk your neck for me. I don't want other Terrae Angeli getting hurt or killed because of me."

"Then stop doing moronic stuff. I won't always be around to save your butt." Without another word, Sergei walked away.

Griffin made a rude gesture that would have gotten him grounded for a week, then headed for lunch. Seeing Basil's door ajar, he paused and peeked in.

His Mentor, dressed in dry clothes, laid stretched out resting on the bed, hands clasped behind his head. He opened his eyes when Griffin stepped in.

"How are you feeling, Basil?"

"I could ask you the same thing." He waved Griffin over.

"Oh, I'm bruised up some." Griffin took a seat on the bed. "And it kind of hurts to breathe, but otherwise, I guess I'm okay."

"Well, you certainly know how to liven up a day. I don't believe I could have slowed your descent without Nan-ja's help. And when I couldn't find you in the pond..." His voice trailed off. He sat up and swung his legs over the edge of the mattress. "Well, no sense in fretting over what might have been. Thanks to Sergei's quick thinking, it all worked out fine, eh?" Basil looped an arm around Griffin's neck and gave him a rough hug.

Griffin endured it for a moment before pulling away.

"Okay, enough with the sappy stuff. Someone's going to walk in and get the wrong idea about us."

Basil let go. "And what idea would that be, Tiro?"

"*That* idea."

"Hmm, I'm not sure I follow you. Please elaborate."

"That we, you know, *like* each other."

"But we do. We have a great deal of affection for each other. In fact, I would say that we love one another."

"Basil!"

"Yes?"

"That is *so* not cool to say that."

"Why?"

"Because we're guys."

"Ah, yes. Whatever was I thinking? Shall I simply punch you, then? Extra credit if I leave a bruise?" Without warning, he swung a cuff at Griffin's head.

Griffin dodged it with a grin and led the way out of the room.

Griffin's Journal: Sunday, May 29th

Let's see: today I almost fell to my death, nearly drowned, and learned that igniting my Fire in mid-flight is a really, really, REALLY bad idea.

Sergei is still being a jerk. When he's not saving my life.

Vassar is way cool.

So is Nan-ja.

And Basil will always be Basil.

Chapter Twenty-One

Basil's Journal: Tuesday, June 7th

Thank heaven, this past week has been fairly un-
eventful. No other near deaths for any of us since Griffin's episode in the pond. Nan-ja has put Griffin and
Sergei through several long training sessions. They have
been too weary by each evening to do more than ex-
change desultory insults across the table. And I must say,
I am impressed with Vassar. She is as tough and skilled
as the boys (as Nan-ja calls them), and in some arenas,
even more advanced.

But all three youths have shown vast improvement,
especially in self-defense techniques. I found myself
hard-pressed to defend against Griffin the other day
when we were Might-sparring. I don't know who was
more surprised: myself or my Tiro.

Sukalli stopped by briefly this evening - still no news
on Nicopolis or how many Lightbringers he's recruited.
I must admit, this enforced exile is beginning to wear
thin.

* * *

"I think I'll just stay here," Griffin mumbled as he lay sprawled on his back in the shallow ditch Vassar had just created. The scent of fresh-churned soil and torn grass filled his nose. "It'll save you the trouble of knocking me down again. No. Really," he added when a shoe nudged his ribs. A shadow fell across him, blocking the noon sun.

"Hey, slacker fish." Vassar grinned down at him. "You realize a female is kicking your butt, don't you?"

"Yeah, but you've had like six years to learn all this extracurricular stuff."

"Excuses, excuses. Now get up."

Griffin reached for her proffered hand. He winced as she pulled him to his feet. Shaking sweat-soaked hair out of his eyes, he faced her again. A few yards away, Sergei practiced sparring Might to Might with Basil while Nan-ja circled around both pairs, coaching. Spotting Griffin upright, she walked over to them.

"Okay, for this next drill, Vassar is going to attack you using Fire. Griffin, I want you to counter-attack using her Element against her."

"How do I do that?"

The Mentor shrugged. "Be creative. Vassar, when you're ready."

Griffin watched as Vassar took a deep breath through her nose. Her body relaxed. The air began to shimmer from the heat building around her. In a blur of movement, she flung out a hand.

KA-WHOOSH! A ball of Fire roared toward his

174

face. Without thinking, Griffin reached up and caught it as if receiving a pass on the basketball court. He let its velocity spin him completely around, heels digging a hole in the ground. Rotating, he picked up speed and shifted the fiery ball into one hand. Coming back around to face Vassar, he pitched it back at her with a flip of his arm, sending it back to her with the help of centrifugal force.

Vassar staggered a step when it slapped into her palms. Cupping her hands around it, she extinguished it. "Nice move."

"Good." Nan-ja nodded in agreement. "Now, let's change it up. I want you two to try to knock each other down. You may only use your Elements. No Might, and certainly no fists or feet."

"Kind of like what we did during our Proeliums?" Vassar asked. Nan-ja nodded.

Griffin hesitated. "I don't know. What if I hurt her?"

Vassar guffawed. "That'll be the day."

"Hey, I might surprise you this time."

Nan-ja smiled. "While your old-fashioned chivalry is charming, Griffin, I assure you Vassar can handle it. Or, would you be more comfortable sparring with Sergei?" Without waiting for his answer, Nan-ja called the Wind and Water angels over. After she explained what she had in mind, Basil agreed.

"By the way, Basil," Nan-ja added with a twinkle in her eyes. "Care to make a wager? I think Griffin will have Sergei flat on his back first."

175

"Oh, bad form, old friend, forcing me to bet against my own Tiro." He studied the two opponents. "What's the wager, by the way?"

"Loser prepares dinner tonight?"

"Agreed." Basil reached over and shook hands with Nan-ja.

"Mentors," Griffin said under his breath.

While Basil and Vassar retired to the shade of the trees bordering the meadow, Griffin and Sergei listened as the petite Mentor gave directions. Afterwards, they walked away from each other, both taking a position a few feet apart. Nan-ja joined Basil and Vassar.

Shifting his weight, Griffin licked dry lips and tried to slow his racing heart as he waited for the signal to begin. *Hope I don't end up on my ass. I don't want to look stupid in front of Basil. Or Vassar.*

"Nervous?" Sergei flexed his hands, blue eyes boring into Griffin's.

"No." *Yes.*

"Get ready to eat some dirt," Sergei said.

"Gee, I think that's my line."

Sergei sneered. "Well, if it will help you get psyched up for this, pretend I'm Nicopolis. And this is your chance for some payback."

"What do you mean?"

Sergei leaned closer and whispered something.

A red haze filled Griffin's vision. "Shut up, you jerk!" Without warning, he punched Sergei in the face. The impact sent a shockwave up his arm. Ignoring it, he

176

threw another punch at Sergei's stomach.

In a downward sweep of his arm, Sergei blocked the second blow as he staggered back. "Wow, you're kind of touchy about that. I was just kidding, you know," he said, rubbing the back of a hand along his jaw. "Don't tell me you're stupid enough to actually believe that?" He squinted at Griffin in surprise. "Wait. You are, aren't you?"

With a snarl of rage, Griffin flung himself at Sergei. Managing to wrap an arm around the other angel's neck, he gave a sharp twist of his body and flipped Sergei over onto his back. Sergei landed on the ground with a thud, dust and dried grass billowing up around him. Breathless, he laid there for a moment, his mouth agape.

Griffin glared down, eyes flashing a brown fire. He started to say something, then stopped and spat to one side. Wiping his mouth, he stalked away.

Ignoring Basil calling to him from across the meadow, Griffin stiff-legged it toward the pond. He paused on the bank, body humming with anger. Clenching and unclenching his fists, he stared unseeing at the far shore.

At that moment, a breath of Wind marred the pond's surface, rippling the water. Basil appeared next to him.

"Fin? Are you alright, lad?"

Griffin nodded and looked away.

"What in heaven's name happened back there? Between you and Sergei?"

"Nothing."

Basil raised an eyebrow.

"Well, nothing you can fix," Griffin amended. "So stop trying to make everything puppies and rainbows for me. I'm a big boy now, you know."

"That you are."

"I have to learn to ignore Sergei and his fat mouth."

"Yes, you do."

"And stop thinking what happened with Nicopolis was somehow my fault."

"A worthy goal."

"To remember that there are others who can help me when I need help."

"Always."

Griffin shook his head. "Don't you *ever* get tired of doing that whole Mentor routine?"

"Never."

In spite of himself, Griffin smiled weakly, some of the fury draining away. He peeked up out of the corner of his eye at the Mentor. Basil's gaze was fixed on the far horizon, his rugged countenance and snow-white hair mirroring the mountains surrounding them.

I wonder if I'll ever become a Mentor and train a Tiro. I never really thought about it before. Heck, I just want to survive my apprenticeship. But maybe some day... His thoughts were interrupted when Nan-ja walked over.

"I say, old chaps, wouldn't this be a good time," she said in a perfect imitation of Basil's accent, "for lunch?"

* * *

"What the heck was that all about?" Vassar joined

Sergei in the middle of the meadow. They watched as Nan-ja sauntered over to the pond.

Sergei threw up his hands. "The kid cannot take a joke. I was just teasing him about his former mentor and he went nuclear on me."

Vassar frowned. "What do you mean?"

"Well, you know the screw-up by Command? Griffin being made mortal and all that?"

"Yeah. Nan-ja told me about that. She also told me that Nicopolis was Griffin's first Mentor. But something went wrong and he was re-assigned to Basil, right?"

"Do you know why?"

"All Nan-ja would say is that there were some problem between Nicopolis and Griffin."

Sergei glanced over his shoulder at the threesome by the pond. He lowered his voice. "Well, I think Nicopolis used to beat him up. Pretty badly."

"Oh, no," she breathed, staring over at Griffin. After a moment, she turned back. "So, what did you say to him?"

"I simply joked that maybe Nicopolis had a reason for doing what he did." He shrugged. "I didn't think he'd take it seriously. I was just kidding around and—"

"You think that's something to joke about?" A look of disgust flowed across her face. She curled her lip. "You're sick."

"Oh, come on. It's not like he isn't one of the top Tiros and—"

"You know something, Sergei?" Vassar's eyes snapped

with fury. "I was really excited when Nan told me about this assignment. I'd heard a lot about you and I was looking forward to working with you. Maybe learn some new techniques. But you've turned out to be the most self-centered, judgmental jack-butt I've ever met. Just when we all could use a real guardian angel, especially Griffin."

"Look, Vassar, I didn't mean to—"

"Seriously. Would it have hurt you to at least be a *friend* to him? Seems like he could use one." She stared to walk away, then spoke over her shoulder. "Talk about an embarrassment to the Terrae Angeli. The only thing worse would be if you were an Earth and Fire." She stormed away toward the lodge.

Sergei stared after her, mouth hanging open. Vassar's words stung his ears. And his heart. He blew out a long breath as he noticed the Mentors and Griffin making their way across the meadow toward him. "See, this is the problem with being a superstar," he muttered. "All this pressure to perform." As they drew nearer, he held up a hand. "May I speak with Griffin in private?"

"No," growled Griffin.

"Yes," Basil said. He took Nan-ja's elbow and continued toward the building, leaving them alone.

Sergei waited until the Mentors were out of earshot before beginning. "Okay, look, Griffin, I have to admit—goading you has become one of my most favorite past times. It's like teasing a pit bull. Seeing how far I can provoke you. I know I shouldn't, but—"

"Then why don't you stop doing it?"

"Why don't you tell me to go to hell?" Sergei retorted. "Seriously, dude. If someone gives you crap in this world, you've got to give it right back, and make them eat it, too." He locked eyes with Griffin. "No matter who it is."

"What do you mean?"

"You know what I mean."

Griffin tightened his jaw and glanced away. "Easy to say, hard to do. Especially when you're a kid and just trying to stay alive," he said, almost to himself.

Vassar's words whispered in Sergei's head. "Well, you're not that kid anymore. You're practically a full-fledged Terrae Angelus with some wicked moves with Fire." He waited until Griffin looked back at him. "And you've got a lot of guts. So stop listening to that voice in your head that says *kick me, I'm a loser*, and start living up to your reputation."

Astonishment spread across Griffin's face. "I-I have a reputation?"

"Nah, not really. I just said that to boost your self-esteem. So. What do you say we end this cold war." He stuck out his hand. "Truce?"

Griffin hesitated. "Well, at least, a ceasefire." He shook on it. "So now what happens?"

"I'm going to teach you how to swim. This whole almost-drowning thing you keep doing is getting old. Plus, it will get Vassar off my case about you. She about tore my head off when I teased you about Nicopolis."

"Really? What else did she say?"

"That stays between her and me."

"Oh, I get it. You're being nice to me to look good in front of her."

A cocky grin lit up Sergei's face. "Well, you don't expect me to become a choir boy overnight."

Chapter Twenty-Two

Basil paced the kitchen. He paused at every turn to peer out the kitchen window over Nan-ja's head.

"Let them work it out between themselves. Go sit down and drink your tea," Nan-ja said, trying to rinse out the teapot while avoiding being stepped on. Ignoring her own words, she looked out as well. "And I wonder what Vassar is doing in the storage shed."

"Hopefully, locating a shovel with which to knock some sense into both their heads," Basil murmured absently. He perked up when the two figures in the meadow began walking toward the lodge. Picking up his mug, he hurried over and took a seat at the table.

A few minutes later, all three youths walked in. Vassar carried several folded bundles of blue and green plastic in her arms.

"Look what I found." She held up a deflated pool raft.

"Excellent!" Nan-ja exclaimed. "Why, Basil and I had just decided that we were all going to take the rest of the afternoon off."

"We did?" Basil lifted an eyebrow.

"He had commented that a cooling swim in the pond would be just the ticket on such a warm day."

"I did?" The other eyebrow rose.

"And those rafts are perfect for you two Earth and Fires."

"So, are swim trunks optional?" Sergei asked the Mentors, an innocent expression on his face.

"Not bloody likely," they said in unison.

"Bummer."

* * *

"I think I found something better than flying." Bobbing face-down on one of the rafts in the center of the pond, Griffin sighed with contentment, toes dangling in the cool water. He glanced over at Vassar floating nearby. Dressed in a one-piece swimsuit the same color as her hair, she gave a thumbs up in agreement. Flopping over onto her stomach, she paddled closer. Her raft bumped into his with a plastic squeak.

"Want to race?" she asked. "Winner gets to drown Sergei.

"Hey, I heard that."

They looked over. Sergei stood on the shore, one finger pressed against the air valve as he inflated the final raft for Nan-ja. After replacing the cap, he laid it on the ground next to her, then headed around the pond toward the log jutting out over the center.

"See? Wind and Waters do have their uses," Griffin said with a grin to Vassar. It faded when he noticed the direction of her glance. Hurriedly, he reached back and tugged his swim trunks up higher over the thin scar angling across his lower back.

"Griffin, I'm sorry. I didn't mean to stare."

"No big deal." Heat rose in his face. He flicked an errant piece of grass from the raft.

"Was...was it from *him?*"

You have no reason to feel shame for what he did to you, lad, said Basil's voice in his head. *You know that. It wasn't you or any weakness or lack of ability that made him treat you so horribly.* Griffin nodded. "Yeah, but, at least there's only one. And Basil thinks it'll fade even more as time goes on."

For several minutes, they floated in self-conscious silence. Then, Vassar raised her eyebrows as she peeked past him toward the shore. "Hey, look over there. But don't act like you're looking."

Griffin eased his head to one side, pretending to be stretching.

Basil and Nan-ja sat shoulder-to-shoulder on the grassy bank, both still in tee shirts and with jeans rolled up past their ankles. Their bare feet rested in the water as they leaned close, deep in conversation. At a remark from Basil, Nan-ja squawked in mock protest. She scooped up a handful of water and splashed his face. He threw his head back and laughed. Then, to Griffin's astonishment, his Mentor reached over and tucked a strand of hair behind Nan-ja's ear.

"I think they're...they're..." Griffin stammered, unable to say it.

"Flirting," Vassar whispered.

The Tiros looked at each other. "Awkward," they said at the same instance.

"Okay, I am officially freaked out." Griffin started paddling toward the far side. "Come on—I'll race you!"

"Hey, wait a sec," Sergei called from over their heads. He stood on the log jutting out into the center of the pond. As they watched, he dived off, parting the water with only the slightest splash; he surfaced between their rafts a moment later. "Want to practice now?" he asked Griffin.

"As good a time as any."

"What are you guys talking about?" Vassar asked.

"Sergei's going to help me improve my swimming. Want to join us?"

She sat up, kneeling on the raft. "I don't know." She nailed Sergei with a stern eye as he treaded water. "Have you decided to stop being a jerk?"

"Absolutely." He held up a hand. "Angel's honor."

Griffin laughed. "Isn't that supposed to be 'Scout's honor'?"

Sergei flashed a cocky grin. "Oh, I'm no Boy Scout."

"That's for sure." Reaching back, Vassar twisted her hair into a ponytail. "Okay, I'm in."

With a lazy, overhand stroke, Sergei led the way to the shallow end of the pond. He waited while the Tiros slipped off their rafts and pushed them out of the way. Standing waist deep in the water, he began with Griffin.

"Okay, get in position like you're swimming."

"But I'll sink."

"I'll hold you up. Look, the trick is to keep going. Your forward movement will counter-act your lack of buoyancy."

With a look of doubt, Griffin stretched out. Sergei placed an arm underneath him. Flailing his arms and kicking his legs, he splashed in place. After a minute, Sergei began walking beside him. As he struggled across the pond, Sergei matched him with a one-armed stroke.

"I'm going to let you go, so keep going," Sergei yelled above the splashing. "No matter what. Even if you start to go down, keep swimming until you reach the far side."

"'Kay," Griffin panted, face tight with concentration. Sergei removed his arm.

Almost instantly, Griffin felt himself sinking. Kicking even harder, he dug cupped hands into the water, trying to pull himself along. Chin barely above the water, he gulped for breath, coughing when he swallowed water and a few drifting weeds. Arm and leg muscles began to burn.

Limbs becoming heavier with every stroke, he fought to keep going. It was as if the Water resented his presence. *It knows I don't belong here*—the strange thought zipped through his head, then disappeared.

His legs sank. To his surprise, his toes touched the bottom. He stood up in the shoulder-deep water, pulse thundering in his ears. Wheezing for breath, he sloshed over to where Basil and Nan-ja stood on the bank, applauding.

"Oh, well done." Basil waded out to meet him. He patted Griffin on the back. "And here comes Vassar."

They both turned to watch Vassar making her way across with a determined grimace on her face. Sergei swam beside her, shouting encouragement. When they reached the shallows, he looped an arm around her waist and pulled her to her feet. She nodded her thanks, gasping for air, then turned and high-fived Griffin.

"Wow, that's hard!" She pulled her ponytail around and wrung it out. "Give me solid ground any day." She rolled her eyes as Sergei made another lap around the pond, his movements like a machine. "Show off," she hollered as he swam past.

"That's right," he called back. "Are you impressed yet?"

Griffin snorted. He started for shore when a gust slapped him in the face. "Hey, knock it off, Basil. You're as bad as Sergei..." His voice faded away when he looked up at his Mentor.

Face tense, Basil scanned the nearby woods. Another gust, higher up, whipped at the tree tops. With a curse, the Mentor turned and thrust Griffin and Vassar toward the shore. "Get over by Nan-ja. Hurry. Sergei—to me," he shouted.

As Sergei vanished from sight, Griffin and Vassar splashed through the knee-high water. They winced when their bare feet made contact with the pebbly ground. Nan-ja took up a defensive position between the Tiros and the meadow. The wind increased, slapping at the grasses and trees and forming miniature white-caps on the pond.

Basil backed out of the water, his eyes searching the surrounding terrain, and joined the others. Sergei appeared next to them. The three Terrae Angeli formed a circle around the Tiros.

The sky darkened as clouds began rolling in from all directions like gray predators. Twigs and gravel whirled through the air and bit at bare torsos and legs. Nearby, pine trees moaned from the assault.

"Make for the lodge," Basil hollered over the storm's fury. "We'll regroup inside!" He snagged Griffin's arm and pulled him to his side. "You stay with me. Sergei, go with Nan-ja and Vassar."

"Like hell," Nan-ja yelled back, dark hair whipping around her head. "Griffin's the prime target, not us. You three go ahead. We'll play rearguard."

"I agree." Sergei took up a position on the other side of Griffin. "Let's roll."

"No!" Griffin struggled in Basil's grip. "I'm not letting anyone get hurt because..."

The air exploded overhead. Lightning stained the clouds with an ugly yellow; ozone soured the air. Before he could argue further, Basil grabbed him by the arm with an iron grip and flung him into the air.

"Fly!"

Griffin flew, Basil and Sergei right behind him. Silence enveloped them. Already muted by flight, the light dimmed as they traveled through the storm.

Materializing on the back porch, Griffin skidded to a halt, slapping his hands against the building to avoid a face plant. Basil and Sergei landed a split second after him. Sergei kicked the door and shoved Griffin inside.

From the doorway, Griffin watched as Sergei took a stance next to Basil while they waited for Nan-ja and Vassar. A moment later, Mentor and her Tiro appeared on the ground below the porch.

"Inside," Basil ordered.

Dashing side by side up the steps, Nan-ja and Vassar darted into the lodge with Sergei on their heels. Basil remained on guard in the open doorway.

With a final rumble, the storm began to abate. The wind died down. Clouds shredded apart and drifted away toward the east, leaving a clear blue sky. Basil waited a while longer before stepping inside and closing the door.

For a long moment, the *plink-plink* of water dripping from soaked hair and clothes filled the kitchen. Then, Griffin spoke. To him, it sounded like somebody else's voice.

"It was Nicopolis, wasn't it?"

Basil nodded. "I'm afraid so, lad. He has found us."

"What's our next move?" Nan-ja asked, pushing wet hair off her face.

"As Sukalli mentioned, this lodge was fortified with Might by Mayla and the rest of Command." Basil glanced around the room. "Supposedly, it should hold off an attack."

"*Supposedly?*" Sergei shook his head. "That doesn't sound good."

Basil shrugged. "It all comes down to the power of the *arba'a* and Nicopolis' ability to wield it. For now, we can only assume that we are under siege."

Chapter Twenty-Three

After flinging on dry clothes, Griffin hurried back out of his bedroom. Vassar and Sergei waited in the hallway, already dressed; Vassar raking fingers through still damp hair.

"Let's go before the party starts without us." Sergei led the way toward the stairs.

They jogged down the stairs and joined the Mentors in the great room. Nan-ja stood in the fading sunlight coming through the western window, scanning the meadow with a pair of binoculars; Vassar took a stand next to her. Basil waited by the open front door. He glanced over a shoulder and caught Griffin's eye.

Griffin joined him. "Any sign?"

"Nary a one."

Something niggled at Griffin. "So, why didn't he just kill us all back at the pond?"

"Because Nicopolis cannot resist a chance to show off. And, as you know from personal experience, he takes a twisted pleasure in creating terror in others. My guess is that he'll play with us first before he attacks. Much like a cat playing with a mouse before the kill."

He's not killing any of you. Not if I can help it, Griffin thought. "Can we defeat him?"

"Of course we can," said a voice behind them. They turned.

Sergei stood there. "We're the good guys, remember? Heavenly warriors against evil and all that. Kind of like Jedi knights, except that we're real." He nodded at Griffin. "You can be Luke Skywalker."

"So, that would make you..."

"Han Solo, of course."

"Of course. And Vassar?"

Sergei made curling motions on either side of his head. He lowered his voice and leaned closer. "Especially if she wore that slave outfit—"

"I can hear you, you know!" yelled Vassar from the other side of the room. They snorted with laughter while Basil shook his head in amusement.

"What about Basil?" Griffin continued, grateful for the brief respite from fear.

"Yoda."

"Ah, I see the resemblance."

"Mock your Mentor, you should not," Basil croaked in a passable imitation.

Sergei stroked his chin. "Now, about Nan-ja..."

The petite Mentor let out a Wookie-like roar.

Over the laughter, Griffin caught a faint ringing from his jean pocket. Still chuckling, he pulled the cell phone out to answer it. Basil protested.

"I don't recall lending you my phone again."

"You didn't. I just forgot to give it back to you."

Griffin stepped over to the dinning area and turned his back on the room before he began speaking. "Hi, you."

"How's it going? Are you okay?" Katie asked, her voice fading in and out.

"Well..." Griffin hesitated, not sure where to start. "Um...let's just say it has not been boring. Lots of training and a few near-death experiences. Plus it looks like Nicopolis has found us."

"Oh, my gosh," she breathed. "Are-are you scared?"

Griffin glanced around before slipping through the swinging doors into the kitchen. He walked to the far corner. "Yeah—a little. Actually, a lot." Relief swept over him at being able to voice the fear.

"Oh, Griffin."

"The thing I'm most freaked about is that someone is going to get hurt or killed because of me. I don't know what to do, Katie. Maybe I *should* just take off. Let Nicopolis follow me and leave the others alone."

"No way—you stay there! And if I find out you're thinking of doing something stupid like leaving, I'm telling Basil."

Griffin snorted. "You would, too."

"You bet I would."

Grinning, he spun a forgotten spoon around on the counter. "So how's your mom and dad? Have you talked with Cas lately?"

"Mom is crazy with worry over you and Basil. Dad, too.

And Cas and I are going to the movies in a few minutes. Just as friends," she added quickly.

He ignored the nip of jealousy. "Good. That's good—I want you guys to hang out, remember?" He looked up when Vassar stuck her head through the swinging doors. "Hold on, Katie."

"Basil wants you," Vassar said, and left.

"Who was that?" Katie asked.

"Vassar. Another Tiro. She and her Mentor, Nan-ja, are here to help us out."

"Oh. I see."

Griffin frowned at the strange note in Katie's voice, then shrugged. "Listen, I've got to go. I'll try to call you this evening."

"I'll be out with Cas, remember? But I'll have my cell on."

"Oh. Right." Over the phone, he heard Bear begin to bark.

"That's Cas. I better go. Now, be careful."

"I will. And I'll try to call—"

The connection closed. He stared at the blank screen. It was several minutes before he could whisper, "Bye, Katie."

* * *

While evening crept into the corners of the lodge, Basil continued the vigil by the front door. Sergei made repeated sweeps of the second floor. Nan-ja leaned a shoulder against the glass as she gazed westward. Stars gleamed in the navy sky over the pass.

In the kitchen, Griffin and Vassar rummaged around,

trying to put together some kind of dinner. Standing in front of the open refrigerator, he scratched his head.

"How about grilled cheese sandwiches and tomato soup? Since it's one of the few things I can make."

"Works for me." Vassar pulled out a loaf of bread from the cupboard. "Plus it's a meal we can all eat—"

KA-BOOM!

A tremor ran through the lodge, rattling the windowpanes. Dishes clattered on the shelves. At Basil's urgent voice and the thudding of running feet, Griffin shot across the kitchen. He burst through the swinging doors, Vassar on his heels.

Sergei stood by the front door, peering out. Cool air wafted through the room. He glanced back as they rushed over to him.

"What the hell was that?" Griffin asked. "Where's Basil?"

"He and Nan-ja went around back to check it out."

"What!" Vassar exclaimed. "Are they crazy?

"That's what *I* asked them, but you know Mentors— they think they're indestructible. Always doing dumb stuff that could get themselves hurt." Sergei said. He stepped out onto the porch and sniffed the air. "It felt like an explosion, but I don't smell any smoke."

"More like a sonic boom," Griffin said. He pushed past Sergei and ran down the steps. "Basil?" he hollered into the night.

Sergei jumped off the porch, followed by Vassar, and grabbed him by the arm. "Where do you think you're going?"

"To help Basil. Now let me go!" He struggled to pull free as Vassar grabbed him by the other arm.

"Sergei's right," she said. "You're staying here until they come back."

"Oh, that may be quite some time," said a voice from the shadows.

They whirled around. Six figures emerged out of the darkness and began walking toward them, gravel crunching under their feet. The foremost one stepped into the rectangle of light spilling from the open door.

Nicopolis.

He stood there in a gray suit out of place in the mountain setting. He gestured toward the other figures. "Come, my fellow Lightbringers." They joined him and formed a circle around the three friends.

Griffin's heart punched against the inside of his chest when he noticed that each of the Lightbringers wore an *arba'a* on silver chains. Varying shades of pale hair declared them all Wind and Waters.

Sergei started forward. Immediately, two of the Lightbringers lifted their hands. With a cry of surprise, he began floating upward. Kicking his legs helplessly, he cursed, then flung out an arm at Nicopolis, palm forward. Nothing happened. A moment later and Vassar joined him in the air.

"Fry them," Sergei snarled at her.

"With pleasure." She snapped her fingers. A single flame flickered once, then died. She tried again with no success.

The ex-Mentor and his followers laughed. "See how easy?" Nicopolis gloated. Sergei and Vassar drifted higher until they were ten feet above the ground. They hovered there like balloons tethered by a string.

"Let them go." Griffin started forward.

"Oh, no, you don't." Nicopolis cut his pale eyes at Griffin. "If you take another step, I will have my colleagues drop your little friends head-first into the ground, making *quite* sure they snap their necks."

"You want me? Fine—you got me." Fear for his friends slashed him like a razor. "But Sergei and Vassar have nothing to do with all this."

"On the contrary. But for now..." Nicopolis flicked a finger.

Griffin gasped. A giant, invisible hand grabbed him and pinned his arms and legs in place. He strained to move, wrenching his head from side to side. The hand tightened.

Nicopolis sauntered over. He lifted the *arba'a* by its chain and dangled it in front of Griffin's nose.

"Talk about a gift from heaven. Actually, many gifts—I found a cache of these in Damascus. It had appeared someone had tried to hide them centuries ago." He swung it back and forth like a pendulum. "With our *arba'as*, my friends and I have unlimited powers."

"*Friends?*" Vassar retorted. "Looks more like some kind of blondes-only, Aryan wannabe club." She glanced at Sergei. "No offense."

"None taken."

"Silence, you disgusting Earth and Fire," spat one of the Lightbringers. His pale hair fell to his shoulders, framing a youthful face. Mouth twisting with hate, he pointed at Vassar and rotated his hand.

With a cry, Vassar flipped around until she dangled upside down. In a sickening jolt, she plummeted to the earth, halting just inches from the ground. Griffin's heart swelled with admiration when she sucked in a deep breath and spoke.

"Hey, watch it. You're getting my hair dirty."

"Wilhelm, leave her be. Now is not the time," Nicopolis ordered. He waited while Wilhelm spun Vassar around and returned her to her original position, then turned back to Griffin.

Griffin lifted his chin and locked gazes with his tormentor. As he battled the old fear welling up, a tiny part of his brain noted that the ex-Mentor was a few inches shorter than him. Lips stiff, he forced a grin.

"What are you smiling about?" Nicopolis snarled

"I was just thinking how short you are. Is that why you're such a monster? Compensation?"

Without warning, Nicopolis struck him across the cheek. Griffin tasted blood. Ears ringing, he shook his head.

Then he spat in Nicopolis' face.

"You vile little beast!"

Stars exploded in his vision as Nicopolis struck him

again and again. Unable to lift his arms to defend himself, his head whipped from side to side with each blow. It seemed to go on forever. Then, the beating stopped. For a moment, a dark haze surrounded him. His head slumped forward.

A blast of icy Water stung his face and shocked him awake. "How dare you spit on me!" Nicopolis plucked a handkerchief from his breast pocket and wiped his chin.

Griffin blinked, trying to focus. "Go to hell," he croaked. *There, Sergei, I finally said it.*

"*Go to hell,*" Nicopolis mimic. He snorted and turned to his followers. "See what I mean about these Earth and Fires? Past time to purge ourselves of these lesser beings. We'll begin with these three. Take them to the mine."

"Even Sergei?" Wilhelm asked. "He's a Wind and Water. Can't he be saved?"

Nicopolis glanced upward "I'm afraid it's too late for him—he's too indoctrinated by now with the idea that Terrae Angeli are created equal."

The Lightbringers all shuddered. Then another one spoke. "And what of the two Mentors? Won't they try to rescue their Tiros?"

"Oh, for certain. They are disgustingly narrow-minded, especially Basil. *Him* we could never hope to turn." He sneered at Griffin. "Which is why several of our more bellicose colleagues are not with us right now. They had a special task to complete."

Nicopolis' face lit up as four other Wind and Water angels, also wearing *arba'as*, materialized in their midst.

All of them sported burns on their faces and clothes. One cradled his arm, shoulder clearly dislocated while another stood hunched over, holding her ribs. "Well?"

The tallest of them, Viking-like in stature, and with a dark blonde beard and shaggy hair, hesitated for a moment before nodding. "Good news, Nicopolis."

"You were successful, then, my good Occum?"

"Yes," Occum replied. "Basil and Nan-ja are no longer a threat. They have fallen."

Chapter Twenty-Four

Claws reached into Griffin's chest with icy fingers and ripped his heart out. Then, a strange nothingness settled over him, as if he were in a fog. Dimly, he heard Sergei yelling with fury, almost drowning out Vassar's wail. He shook his head in confusion. *Basil dead? No, something's wrong. He can't die. He's* Basil, *for heaven's sake.*

He staggered a step when the invisible force released him. Immediately, two tall Lightbringers grabbed him and dragged him between them. He struggled, almost breaking free, before one of them grabbed him by the hair and yanked his head back.

"Give me a reason," the Lightbringer said in a low voice.

Digging cruel fingers into his arms, their combined Might overpowered him. With a lurch, he was yanked into the night sky by his captors.

They headed west toward the mountain pass, the stars overhead a blur. Behind him, he could hear Vassar sobbing. Twisting his head around, he spotted her hair, a flame against the silvery light. Further back, Sergei fought a running battle with his own guards.

A few minutes later, they materialized inside a rocky tunnel scarcely head height. The damp air smelled stale, leaving an acerbic taste on his tongue. Several old-fashioned lanterns hung from abandoned mining pikes driven into cracks. The lamps' flames flared each time another team with their captive appeared. Nicopolis arrived last. Holding up his *arba'a* with one hand, he began dragging his other hand up and down the rock face of the tunnel.

"Sheesh, get a dog if you want to pet something," Sergei said. Griffin noticed he had a battered eye and a cut along his chin. *I bet he fought them the entire flight.*

"It would probably run away," Vassar pointed out, eyes red from weeping, but her voice steady and strong.

"Or bite him," Griffin added in support. "Of course, it might get rabies or something."

"Silence them, Occam." Nicopolis said over a shoulder as he continued the strange ritual. "I cannot concentrate."

The bearded giant grabbed Vassar by the throat with a massive paw. He drew back a fist when Griffin and Sergei started forward. "One more step and I'll damage this lovely face," Occam said in a matter-of-fact voice. "And by the way, your Elements and use of Might are null and void in here thanks to the power of our *arba'as*. Back off."

Griffin and Sergei exchanged frustrated glances and eased back. For a few minutes, the only sound was the echo of Nicopolis' voice as he muttered under his breath. Vassar stood ramrod straight, eyes flashing with an amber fire as she glared up at Occam.

Finally, Nicopolis finished. "There. That should be sufficient," he said, dusting his hands.

He plucked a lantern from the nearest pike and led the way downward into the darkness. The other Lightbringers herded the three friends together and boxed them in front and rear. They stumbled along the almost pitch-black tunnel as it twisted and turned. Ahead of them, Nicopolis' lantern bobbed in and out of view.

"Hey, are you okay," Griffin whispered to Vassar walking beside him.

"Oh, just peachy," she whispered back. "I'm keeping my spirits up imagining what I'm going to do to Thor up there," she gestured toward Occam, "when I get a chance." She slipped her hand into his. "Griffin, do you really think they're...you know. Nan-ja and Basil?"

He squeezed. "Of course not," he lied. To Vassar and to himself. "Nicopolis is just saying that to freak us out. To hurt us."

"That's what I think, too. And until I learn different, I'm going to keep believing they're alive." She let go and eased back to speak with Sergei.

Griffin walked along, one hand touching the narrow passageway's wall for balance. *He can't be dead. Because I'm not ready to lose him. Maybe years from now, but not yet. I have too much to learn from him. Too much to say to him. I just hope it's not too late.*

* * *

203

Tossed by the guards onto the rocky floor of a small alcove, Griffin rolled over, then scrambled out of the way as Sergei and Vassar landed in a heap beside him.

He clambered to his feet. Looking around, he examined their surroundings in the flickering light of Nicopolis' lantern. A narrow opening, complete with a jail-like door, separated the alcove from the tunnel. Century-old timbers held up the ceiling. With a clang, the door swung shut.

"Welcome to the Orphan Boy Mine," Nicopolis said as he peered through the iron bars. "An appropriate name, given the recent turn of events. It was abandoned over a hundred years ago when the gold rush died out." He reached up and patted the bars. "And while ordinary iron and rock would not detain even a sub-par Terrae Angelus as yourself, you will find that I've made some special modification to your prison. In fact, to this entire mine. I have strengthened the rock walls as well as this door with Might using my *arba'a*." He smiled at Griffin's look of dismay. "Oh, yes. Not only does this little device increase *my* abilities, it also allows me to extend my Might's power to objects. In essence, I have created a Terrae Angelus-proof prison cell. Neither flight nor your Elements will free you from it."

Despair clawed at him. "What are you going to do to us?"

"Oh, nothing at this moment. But, at dawn, you three will be our guests of honor at an inaugural event."

"What's he talking about?" Sergei said as he and

Vassar joined Griffin.

Nicopolis stroked a finger along the lock. "You see, while in exile, I thought a great deal about why I had been treated so disgracefully by my kind, and why the once mighty and noble Terrae Angeli have become more *Terrae* and less *Angeli*. Then, one night, I had an epiphany. It was almost like divine inspiration." He flicked the *arba'a*. "And with the discovery of these, I knew my plan must be sanctioned by God Himself."

"What plan?"

Nicopolis pressed his pale face between the bars, stretching the skin on either side. His eyes bulged slightly. "Why, I am going to purify the Terrae Angeli. Starting with a certain filthy little Earth and Fire." He cut his eyes toward Vassar. "Or two."

"What about me?" Sergei asked. "Don't I get invited to the party?"

Nicopolis pulled away. "Oh, I had toyed with the idea of offering you a position in my new order, but I can already see that you are too..." He waved his hand about with a vague gesture.

"Loyal?" Sergei said. "Gallant? Stunningly handsome?"

"Polluted," Nicopolis said, "by overexposure to these kind. Of course, being raised by an Earth and Fire, you weren't brought up with the proper understanding of the natural hierarchy." At their expressions of confusion, Nicopolis elaborated. "Our kind," he swept an arm around to include the followers behind him, "are closer

205

to Heaven by the simple fact that we are Wind and Water. The *pristine* Elements. The *unsoiled* Elements. The—"

"So, what's your plan," Griffin interrupted.

Nicopolis beamed as if sharing a secret. "I intend to re-make our entire order into what it should be. An order of angels to rival even the celestial ones."

"And you think *I* have delusions of godhead," Sergei muttered out of the corner of his mouth to Griffin.

"What do you mean," Vassar asked, "by *purify?*"

"Why, eliminate every Earth and Fire, of course. As well as any Wind and Waters who do not agree with us." He spun on his heels. "Which reminds me, I have preparations to make." Humming to himself, he strolled back up the tunnel, taking the lantern with him. His followers marched along behind him, the echo of their footsteps fading away.

Darkness engulfed their prison. Griffin held up his hand and flicked the tip of a finger against his thumb. A tiny flame sputtered, then went out. "Almost got it." Sucking in a deep breath, he snapped his fingers as hard as he could.

Fire flared to life. Gritting his teeth from the effort, Griffin stood in the middle of the cell and held his arm aloft, thumb stuck out as if he were hitchhiking. "I think I can keep this going for awhile," he said. "Spread out and see if you can find a way out of here."

They walked around the perimeter of their confine, scarcely ten feet across, peering into every crack and crevice. Vassar managed to get a finger lit. She squatted down and examined the junction between the bars and the rocky ground. "Hey, guys, I think these bars are just jammed against the floor, not buried into it. Which means we might be able to punch our way out, even with all this *arba'a* mumbo-jumbo crap." She looked over her shoulder at Griffin. "I mean, we did get our Fire going. Kind of."

Griffin knelt beside her. A sudden wave of dizziness engulfed him. Leaning over, he pressed his forehead against the cold bars as his pulse hummed in his ears.

"You okay?" she asked.

"Yeah. Just lightheaded. That *arba'a* stuff really screws up my Elements."

"Mine, too." Vassar shifted her position. "Listen, why don't you try first? Extinguish your Fire so you're not wasting energy. I can keep mine going."

"Good idea." Flexing his hands several times, he eyed the ends of the bars wedged against the ground. After a few minutes, he nodded. "Okay, I think I'm ready. Here goes." He took a deep breath, then punched his fist into the floor next to the jail wall.

A white-hot pain shot up his arm. "Oh, Fire," he moaned, slumping over and cradling the injured limb. Gasping, he blinked back tears of agony. "Son of a..." He stopped himself in time.

"That has *got* to hurt," Sergei said, taking a knee on the other side of him. He peered down at the spot Griffin had hit and shook his head. "Nope, we're not getting out that way."

Staggered to his feet, he flexed his throbbing wrist. "You think?" he snapped, then dragged his other hand down his face, wincing at the bruises. Licking his lips, he swallowed, suddenly aware of a dry mouth. Cocking his head at a trickling noise, he followed the sound over to the back corner of the cave.

A dribble of underground water seeped down the side of the rock face. It gathered into a shallow indentation on the floor before disappearing into a nearby crack.

Griffin crouched down and pressed his mouth to the pool. He slurped up a tiny mouthful and swallowed. *Hmm, tastes okay—just a little gritty.* "You guys thirsty?"

"Is there water?" Vassar walked over, her flame flickering. A sheen of sweat covered her face from the effort to keep her Fire going. "Because there's no way I'm drinking anything coming out of Sergei's fingers. I mean, when was the last time he washed his hands?"

"Ha, ha. Very funny." Sergei took Vassar's elbow and helped her kneel down to drink. "By the way, I tried a few minutes ago to get either of my Elements to work. I could generate enough Wind to blow out a birthday candle, but that's about it."

"Vassar, why don't you take a break? We can be without light for awhile," Griffin suggested. "In fact, maybe we should all rest a bit, have some water, and then try again."

Drying her mouth on the sleeve of her hoodie, Vassar sighed with contentment. "Oh, wow, I needed that." She scooted aside, her flaming hand still up in the air,

208

and joined Griffin as he leaned back against the wall. After drinking his fill, Sergei took a seat on the other side of Vassar. With a groan of relief, she extinguished the Fire and dropped her hand.

Blackness engulfed them. They sat side by side in silence, lost in thought, all of them dozing off and on as the night crept past. The *ker-plunk* of each measured drop refilling the pool was magnified by the dark.

Jerking awake several hours later, Griffin pulled his knees to his chin. Despair began to eat at him, sinking its teeth into his chest. *Oh, God, don't let be true. Please.* He ground his forehead against his knees, eyes squeezed tight as he shoved the fear back down. *I know what Basil would say—keep the faith.*

Next to him, Vassar sniffed and sniffed again. Her shoulder bumped his as she reached back and pulled her hood down over her head. Beyond her, Sergei stirred. A moment later, Griffin felt him drape an arm around Vassar, stretching out enough to also lay a hand on Griffin's shoulder. They sat united for a long minute. Then, Sergei cleared his throat.

"Listen," he said. "We need to get out of here and warn Flight Command. Plus, I don't think I want to wait around for what Adolf Junior's got planned for us." He untangled himself and pushed up. "Which one of you wants to play Zippo lighter?"

"I'll do it." With a grunt, Griffin snapped his fingers. As the flame began dancing on his thumb, he rose, followed by Vassar.

"Let me know when you need a break," she said, pushing the hood back. "We'll take turns."

Griffin nodded and lifted his arm. Suddenly, the Fire flared up, illuminating his friends' faces with a golden glow. He raised his arm higher and stretched it up as high as he could. The flame flickered wildly. "I think there's a draft coming from up there." He pointed with his other hand toward the low roof of their cell.

Above their heads, almost invisible against the coal-black rock, was a shadow. As Griffin stepped closer and stood on his toes, the shadow became a hole.

Sergei joined him. "Could be a way out or it might just a dead end." He grabbed the lip of the hole and chinned himself up, toes scrabbling for purchase. "It's too dark for me to see anything, but I think I smell water." He lowered himself and waved Vassar over. Taking a knee like a football player, he formed a platform with his leg and patted it. "Climb up and take a look."

Vassar clambered up on Sergei's knee. With one hand clutching the top of Griffin's head for balance, she ignited a finger and thrust it into the hole. For a long minute, she peered inside.

"Well?" Griffin said.

"Sergei's right. I see a big pool—that must be where the trickle of water's coming from." She tensed. "Oh, wow!"

"What?" Griffin and Sergei asked at the same time.

"I think I see a few stars and the silhouette of trees on the far side. It looks like maybe there's another mine entrance on the far side of the pool." Vassar leaned further in the hole. Her voice echoed. "Yup, there's a strong breeze; it smells like fresh air." With a nimble twist, she leaped down. "I think we can squeeze through this hole. I can, for sure, but you two might—"

The sound of approaching footsteps, punctuated by a metallic clinking sound, ran along the tunnel toward them. A beam of light bobbed along the walls. As they stood frozen, Nicopolis' disembodied voice spoke, growing louder with each second.

"And I want them chained together, but not too close. With *him* last. That way, he can watch his friends die before him."

Chapter Twenty-Five

"Move!" Griffin grabbed Vassar and hoisted her back up. "Just shut up and get out of here," he barked when she started to argue. As she wiggled headfirst into the hole and disappeared, Sergei leaped to his feet.

He cupped his hands, forming a stirrup for Griffin. "You next, bro," he said, the faint light from the approaching lantern casting half his face in shadow.

Griffin hesitated for a moment before placing a foot in Sergei's clasped hands and reached for the hole. A pair of hands seized his wrists. With Vassar pulling and Sergei pushing, he squeezed through, tearing tee shirt and losing skin on both shoulders. He dropped down a few feet onto a rocky ledge; a wide pool lapped at the edge of it. Next to him, Vassar gave a snap and lit her Fire. He turned back.

"Sergei," he hissed, afraid to yell any louder.

"I'm coming—don't wet your pants." Sergei's hands appeared, then his head, pale hair gleaming in the light from Vassar's flame. Griffin grabbed his arms and yanked as hard as he could.

"Hey, watch it!" Sergei complained as his back raked

along the rough edge of the hole. He slithered through and landed on one knee next to Vassar. "Quick," he said softly, "put out your Fire."

Vassar clenched her fist. They huddled down in the dark, holding their breaths as the lantern's light grew brighter. A moment of silence. Then a multitude of voices began shouting all at once. Nicopolis screeched orders. Metal clanged against metal as the cell door was flung open.

"Hurry. While they're trying to figure out where we went." Griffin lowered himself into the pool, trying to remember how to breathe as his whole body rebelled from the snowmelt water. Clutching the rocky shelf with one hand, he waited until his feet touched the bottom. "Okay, it's only waist deep," he whispered through clenched teeth. "Hurry."

Vassar slipped in next with a gasp of shock. Sergei muttered something about wimpy Earth and Fires as he joined them.

Using the raging voices from the other side to cover any splashing noises, they began wading slowly forward. The inky water was the same shade of black as the mine. Trying not to trip over unseen rocks and old mining tools, they sloshed along. On the far side, a lopsided rectangular shape framed a few stars and the outline of pine trees.

Halfway across, a beam of light shot out from the hole behind them and began sweeping from side to side.

"Underwater. Quick," Sergei hissed.

Bending his knees, Griffin gulped a mouthful of air, then sank. Swimming clumsily, he pulled himself along the bottom, hoping he was going in the right direction. Beside him, Sergei's legs churned like a blender as he dragged Vassar along with one arm. They pulled ahead of Griffin.

Lungs burning, Griffin crawled the final yards on hands and knees. He gasped as his head broke the surface. Two sets of hands grab his arms and yanked him to his feet.

Without looking back, the threesome scrambled over the stone-littered ground. They dashed through the doorway, passing between rough timbers sagging away from each other, and ducked to one side.

Griffin eased around one of the timbers and peeked back inside. "I don't see any light."

"Do you think they saw us?" Vassar asked, her teeth chattering.

"Don't know," Griffin said. "But we've got to get moving."

He gazed around. Small rocks and gravel fanned out from the doorway for several yards; leftover debris from decades of mining. A few weeds and one brave pine tree struggled to grow in the tailings. In the valley below, the lodge looked like a discarded toy.

Griffin glanced back up the mountainside, craning his head. A second entrance gaped at them a hundred yards further up the slope. *I bet that's where we first came in.*

He shivered when the night breeze found his wet clothes. Out of habit, he tensed his body. Warmth spread from his chest. Steam began rising from shirt and jeans

"Whoa." Vassar laid a hand on his arm. "You got your mojo back." Dropping her hand, she squeezed her eyes tight. Her soaked hair began to curl and thicken. Opening her eyes, she grinned at Griffin. He grinned back. They both flinched when a blast of Wind stung their faces.

"Excellent," Sergei said, lowering an arm. "Good to know the *arba'a*'s power is limited."

"Then we've got a chance," Vassar said.

"A chance for what?" asked Griffin.

"We need to get back to the lodge and grab a cell phone or find some other way to contact Command."

"You realize that will be the first place Nicopolis will look for us, don't you," Sergei said.

"Not if we hurry," Vassar said. "We only need like a minute. My phone is in my desk drawer. We'll fly in a full speed, grab it, and be out of there before they know we're there."

Sergei raised his eyebrows. "How are you two *Tiros* at landing *inside* a building?"

"As good as you," Griffin said.

"Yeah, right. I've seen you in action."

Vassar snorted in disgust. "Knock off with the male posturing crap. We need to get out of here. Let's fly down to the trees by the pond. Meet by that big pine near the western edge? We'll stay out of sight while we take a

215

look around, then decide on our next move. Agreed?"

Griffin shrugged. "Fine by me."

"Right. Meet you guys there."

Vassar vanished in a warm gust of air. Griffin and Sergei followed. They reappeared a few minutes later next to a massive spruce. Keeping the thickest trees between themselves and the lodge, they skirted the pond. When they reached the edge of the forest, they crouched down behind the last pine and peered through its branches. To the east, the stars had already faded.

"I don't see any lights or movement," Sergei said, craning his neck. "Of course, that doesn't mean anything. Nicopolis could still—"

"Hey," Griffin interrupted him. "I smell smoke."

Their eyes snapped to the top of the chimney. A pale tendril curled out, barely noticeable against dawn sky. The sound of a door slamming shut echoed from the far side of the building; a voice called and was answered by another.

Griffin stiffened at the voice. The hairs on the back of his neck stood at attention. He shuffled forward on his knees, trying to get a closer look, then rose when the back door opened. A tall figure stepped out.

"We're too late," Vassar said. "They're already here." She looked at Sergei in dismay.

"Guess we're going to have to find another way to contact—" Sergei began.

Griffin never heard the rest of the sentence. He burst out from cover at a dead run. Ignoring Sergei's *what the hell are you doing,* he sprinted toward the lodge.

At the sound of the shout, the figure paused, then hurried down the wooden steps toward him, a figure with a white bandage covering the left side of his face.

Griffin pumped his legs. With each stride, the night's fear slipped away. Halfway across the meadow, he leaped into the air. Landing with a grunt, he skidded to a stop on the gravel path.

And flung himself into Basil's arms.

Chapter Twenty-Six

For a long minute, Griffin kept his forehead pressed against the Mentor's chest. "I thought you were dead." He swallowed, fighting for control.

"Clearly, I'm not." Basil patted his back.

"That's what they told Nicopolis," he said hoarsely. Stepping back, he swiped at his face, wondering why he didn't feel more embarrassed.

"Then they lied. Probably out of fear of what he would do to them." He let go and laid his hands on Griffin's shoulder, studying him. "Are you alright, Fin? How did you get those bruises..." His blue eyes narrowed. "Was it Nicopolis?"

Griffin nodded. His jaw dropped when Basil swore. *I can't believe he even* knows *that word, much less would use it.*

"And where's Vassar and Sergei?" As Griffin started to answer, a double *thump-crunch* of feet marked his friends' landing.

Before Vassar could ask the question, Basil called over his shoulder at the open door. "Nan-ja, she's safe." He and Griffin stepped to one side as the Tiro darted past them and hurried inside. Cries of delight followed.

"Listen, Basil," Sergei began, following Mentor and apprentice as they climbed the stairs to the porch. "Nicopolis and his buddies are probably right behind us. They are all packing *arba'as* and on some bizarre crusade."

"What kind of crusade?" Nan-ja stepped out, one arm around Vassar's waist. Her other arm was cradled in a sling.

Sergei hastily recounted the events to the Mentors. When he finished, he asked, "What about Flight Command? Have they been notified?"

"They have," Basil said. "And Sukalli is already—"

At that moment, an almighty wind blasted them. Sukalli appeared a few feet away, the force of his landing sending a shockwave through the porch's decking. Under the heels of his cowboy boots, a fissure split open with a groan. His face was tight and his black eyes snapped with anger.

"Uh-oh," Sergei whispered to Griffin and Vassar. "Somebody's on the warpath."

"Dude, that is *so* politically incorrect," Vassar hissed back.

"Oh, I don't know," the Guardian said as he stomped over and rested a boot on the lowest step. "I think it fits my mood right fine. Somebody bring me up to speed about what that coyote is planning." After Basil filled him in, the Guardian looked from angel to angel, assessing the damage. "Broken arm?" he asked Nan-ja.

"Sprained wrist. Should be fine in a few hours."

"You three pups?"

They looked at each other and shrugged. "Just some cuts and bruises. Nothing a bit of Might-healing can't take care of," Griffin said.

"And you, brother." Sukalli's gaze locked on Basil. "How bad."

"Bearable."

"Did you lose it?"

"It appears so."

"Lose what?" Griffin asked.

Basil hesitated before answering in a matter-of-fact voice. "My left eye."

A wave of dizziness swept over Griffin as the color drained from his face. He sagged against the railing.

"Steady on, Fin. It's not that bad."

"*It's not that bad?*" Griffin's voice cracked. Guilt punched him in the gut. He forced himself to look at his Mentor's face. As punishment.

"Get a grip, Tiro," Sukalli growled. "Ain't nuthin' you could've done. Right now, we've got a band of outlaws coming for us."

"Is Command sending any more to help?" Vassar asked.

"'Fraid not, missy. Every Terrae Angeli we pull out of the field means one less guardian angel for mortals. It's just us six."

Sergei groaned. "Against almost twice that number."

"Why, then, they haven't a chance," Nan-ja said. "Tell you the truth, I'm looking forward to a rematch with..."

She paused and pointed up the valley. "And speak of the devil." The others whirled around.

Clouds began forming over the western pass. Pouring down the mountainside like an approaching avalanche, they filled the valley as they sped toward the lodge. Overhead, the sun dimmed. A false twilight followed.

Kaaa-RRRACK!

Lightning speared the chimney. With a boom, it exploded. Boulders blew apart in all directions. One enormous piece of granite soared up into the air, flipped over in slow motion, and plummeted straight down toward the group.

Nan-ja and Vassar dove off the top step and vanished. One foot still on the bottom tread, Sukalli reached up, grabbed Sergei by the arm, and yanked him off the porch. They disappeared amidst falling shards.

With a shout, Griffin shoved Basil backwards toward the edge of the porch. "Go!" Vaulting one-handed over the railing, he followed the Mentor just as the boulder crashed down. Dodging pieces of splintered decking, they threw themselves into the storm.

Leaning forward as he flew, Griffin squinted, trying to see through the silver veil of flight, the rain stinging his eyelids. On his left, Basil appeared out of the clouds.

Crowding close, the Mentor shouted in his ear. "Make for that cliff. There's a clearing at its base." He pointed at a nearby tower of granite pushing up through the fog, its pinkish color muted by the storm.

Griffin nodded. When Basil released him, he slowed. The mist thickened as he descended between tips of the pines poking up like green fingers.

Basil's shout of warning vied with another clap of thunder.

A hand grabbed his ankle. With a cry, Griffin kicked out with the other foot. Scissoring his legs, he struggled to break free.

"I've got him," yelled a voice in triumph. Griffin looked down.

Wilhelm flew below him, one hand gripping his leg and the other hand clasping the *arba'a*. Pale hair streamed behind him like wings on a Norseman's helmet. Baring his teeth in a wolfish grin, he yanked.

Jerked to a stop in mid-air, Griffin's teeth clicked together. Eyes watered from a bitten tongue. At that moment, Wilhelm grabbed his other leg, flipped him upside down, and thrust him toward the ground.

Flailing his arms, Griffin managed to twist himself around, desperate to land feet first. Panic burned in his throat as the ground rushed upward to meet him. Wind shrieked in his ears. At the last minute, a hand snagged the back of his tee shirt. The collar tightened. He clawed at it as it bit into his throat, choking him.

"Nicopolis doesn't want you to crash and burn just yet," Wilhelm hissed in his ear as they wove in and out of the pines; branches raked Griffin, needles stinging his face and arms. They dropped lower toward the clearing. "But, he never said anything about a few bruises." With a cold laugh, the Lightbringer let go several yards above the ground.

Hitting the ground, Griffin tried to remember to roll as Nan-ja had taught him. Sharp rocks and dead branches clawed him as he tumbled through the grass before crashing to a stop against the cliff face. For several minutes, he laid in a heap, ears humming from the force of the impact. Curses and shouts and the sound of blows made him lift his head. The world spun around him. With a groan, he pushed himself up to his knees.

On the far side of the clearing, Basil and another Lightbringer, nose gushing blood, circled each other. When Wilhelm landed next to Griffin, the Lightbringer snarled over his shoulder.

"You keep that filth from running off," he ordered. Red droplets flew from his mouth as he spoke, the rain darkening his blonde hair. "I'll deal with this one."

"No problem, Titus." Wilhelm stepped behind Griffin.

He winced when Wilhelm yanked him to his feet and pinned his arms back. Pain tore through his arm sockets.

"Try anything and I'll break them," he warned, twisting Griffin's arms higher between his shoulder blades. "And, with the power of my *arba'a*, I can snap them with just a twitch of a finger."

Practically standing on tiptoe, Griffin watched as Basil and Titus squared off. The Mentor angled his head to keep the remaining eye locked on his opponent.

"I must apologize for breaking your nose. I had assumed your *arba'a* would provide better protection." He gestured toward the device hanging from a chain around Titus' neck. "Perhaps you should request your money back."

Titus sneered. "Oh, I haven't even *begun* to use the power this thing gives me. I just need more practice." With a shout, he thrust out his hands, palms forward.

Dropping to one knee, Basil ducked as Titus' Might passed over his head. It plowed into a massive spruce behind him. With a groan, the tree toppled over, its roots flailing the air. It crashed into a grove of aspens and demolished several smaller trees.

Still kneeling, Basil swung his arm in a perfect cricket pitch. Mud and water sprayed out when Titus hit the ground a second later, splattering both combatants. Before his opponent could rise, the Mentor leaped to his feet and pointed.

Water shot from Basil's fingertips. Walking closer, he hosed the Lightbringer with the stream, churning Titus over and over in a tangle of arms and legs. He drove him across the clearing, making sure he slammed the Lightbringer into every rock and log along the way. Reaching the edge of the clearing, he turned off the Element with a snap of his wrists.

As Titus lay moaning on the ground, the Terrae Angelus grabbed his opponent's shirt in both fists and hauled the wobbly Lightbringer upright. "Mind your head," Basil said politely.

Then, to Griffin's astonishment, his Mentor stepped back on his heels, lifted Titus clear off his feet, and began whirling in a circle, dragging the Lightbringer along with him as if he were competing in a hammer-throwing contest—with Titus as the hammer. Faster and faster they spun. After the fourth rotation, Basil let go.

The Lightbringer soared out of sight into the fog. A minute later, the sound of snapping tree limbs echoed faintly through the clearing.

Wilhelm gasped in shock. Griffin felt the grip on his wrists slacken. With a grunt, he tore loose and drove his elbow backwards into Wilhelm's face. A cry of agony followed.

Griffin spun around, hands raised and ready for battle. He grinned at the sight of the young Lightbringer bent over, palm pressed against his mouth. Blood trickled down his chin.

Straightening up, Wilhelm wrapped a bloodied hand around the *arba'a*. "I'm going to freaking *end* you!" He took a step, then froze when he spied Basil striding toward them. Cursing, he leaped into the air and vanished.

"Whoa!" Griffin gawked at his Mentor. "I didn't know you could fight like that. Where did you learn that move?"

Basil shrugged. "Scotland." Before Griffin could ask for details, he continued. "Frankly, we were fortunate those two hadn't had much practice using their *arba'as*." He walked over to the cliff face and leaned against it.

"No kidding." Griffin flexed his aching shoulders as

he joined him. "What do we do now?" He winced when Basil tore the mud-streaked and now useless bandage off his injured eye.

Scrapping at the sodden ground with the heel of his shoe, Basil dug a hole and buried it. "We need to find the rest of our group. If the fighting abilities of the other Lightbringers are anything like the two we just encountered, then our friends should be able to hold their own. At least for awhile." Pulling a handkerchief out of his pocket, Basil folded it on the diagonal, creating a long strip of fabric which he tied at an angle around his head, covering the wound.

Griffin looked away, skin crawling at the sight of the injury. "This is all my fault."

"I beg to differ."

"Beg all you want, Basil. But it's my fault everyone's in danger and you—"

"Griffin."

"—lost an eye. An *eye*! Fire, how many more Terrae Angeli are going to be—"

"Griffin!"

"—injured or killed because of me." He clenched his fists. "Maybe if I give myself up, Nicopolis will take it out on me and leave the rest of you alone."

"That is quite possibly the most ludicrous thing you've ever said, Tiro. And while I appreciate the sacrificial gesture, your death at his hands would not change Nicopolis or his plans. No, he has declared his true intentions. You would simply be the first of many victims."

Slumping against the rock face, Griffin sighed. Exhaustion pulled at him—even his teeth felt weary. "You should have just let me die. The night Mayla turned me mortal. Then none of this would have happened."

"I quite agree," said a voice.

Chapter Twenty-Seven

A figure emerged out of the fog. Nicopolis.

A second figure joined him in the clearing. "See? I told you they were here." Wilhelm's upper lip was split and swollen.

"Bloody..." began Basil.

"...hell," Griffin finished. They started forward.

"Not so fast." Holding the *arba'a*, Nicopolis raised his hand. In a savage movement, he clenched it into a fist.

Griffin winced as the invisible force captured him again. It squeezed tighter, reminding him of every bruise and cut. Next to him, Basil struggled to free himself.

Four others, including a limping and battered Titus, and led by Occam, appeared. They spread themselves in a half circle around Griffin and Basil, crowding them against the cliff.

Nicopolis took a stance in front of them. "Basil—back from the dead. I was informed you had been killed." Nicopolis cut his eyes at Occam and glowered for a moment. Occam shifted his feet nervously. "Ah, well. Life is one unending list of disappointments." Lifting the *arba'a* hanging around his neck, he jiggled the chain. "I assume by now, my old friend, you know what this is?"

"A dog license?" Basil said. "Oh, forgive me—you were being serious." Griffin stifled a laugh.

Nicopolis' mouth twisted. "You two are just alike. What with your flippant quips and devil-may-care attitude."

"That's right, we are," Griffin said. He raised his chin, ignoring the molten fear churning his gut.

"Then, it will be fitting for you to die together."

Basil narrowed his eye. "You would truly murder fellow Terrae Angeli in cold blood? Have you fallen that far?"

"Why, it appears I have," Nicopolis said gleefully. "It's quite freeing, in a way, to embrace purity and my higher calling. After all, I have nothing to lose." He flicked a finger.

Might punched Griffin in the chest, flinging him backwards through the air. With a groan, he smashed against the cliff. Jagged rocks bit into his back. Pinned in place, his feet dangled a yard above the muddy ground, arms outstretched on either side. Straining to free himself, he managed to pull his head loose before Nicopolis gestured again and slammed it back.

"Let him go, Nicopolis!" Basil shouted.

"Now, would I do that? I want him to have a front row seat where he can watch your body dissolve into a puddle at his feet."

"Then, why don't we make it a proper spectacle and

duel it out Might to Might? If the *arba'a* is truly that powerful, you should have no trouble defeating me."

Nicopolis snorted. "Do you think I'm dim-witted? I already have the advantage over you. No, you stay right there where I can kill you without having to roll about in the muck like a filth-covered Earth and Fire. Unlike some, *I* have standards." He glared at Titus who wilted in place.

"You realize Flight Command now knows all about your plan. Even if you murder us, they will send others against you. In the end, nothing will come of all this, but your defeat." Basil looked at the other Lightbringers. "And the defeat of your misguided followers."

"Oh, please, Basil. Spare us your melodramatic speech." Nicopolis turned to the others. "My brothers," he said, raising his voice in triumphant. "This moment is just the beginning of a new era for the Terrae Angeli. An era in which we rid ourselves of all undesirables as well as those who would protect them."

When Nicopolis finished speaking, Titus hobbled forward. One arm dangled uselessly by his side. Hatred twisted his features into an ugly mask. With difficulty, he scooped up a handful of mud and flung it in Basil's face.

Spitting to one side, the Mentor cleared his mouth. "By the fact that you still have one good arm, it appears I didn't throw you far enough."

Titus snarled and took a step closer. Nicopolis pushed him back toward the other Lightbringers. "Enough. We need to finish this." He stared up at the tall Mentor, his pale face aglow with anticipation. "So, Basil. Any final words?"

"Not for you." He turned his head and looked at Griffin. "Steady now, Fin. It will be all right."

Fighting back the panic and horror clawing at his insides, Griffin forced himself to smile. "Promise?"

"I promise." Basil smiled back. "God be with you, son."

"And also with you." His heart tore in two when Nicopolis laid a hand on Basil's chest.

"Close your eyes, lad."

Griffin shook his head, digging fingertips into the rock behind him. Determined to stand vigil.

Nicopolis began the litany. The words filled the air like the stench of a newly dug grave. Thunder rumbled overhead as if the sky was protesting.

Like vultures around a kill, the other Lightbringers crowded forward, pushing each other in their eagerness. After a long minute, the ex-Mentor dropped his hand and stepped back.

Freed from the grip of the *arba'a*, Basil staggered a step. He swayed, then crashed to his knees. Struggling to stay upright, he braced a hand on the ground, features drawn with pain. He raised his face to the heavens and murmured something. His arm gave out.

It seemed to Griffin it took forever for Basil to fall.

Chapter Twenty-Eight

Blackness shrouded Griffin.

Faint shouts of celebration and vague shapes moving to and fro tugged at the edge of his consciousness. He squeezed his eyes shut and tried to burrow deeper into the darkness, desperate for oblivion. The vision of Basil's body falling to the mud-soaked ground looped over and over in his mind.

Pain yanked him back into focus. He gasped as he was dragged down the rocky wall until his feet almost touched the earth. Warm blood trickled down his back from cuts made by a protruding corner of granite.

"There, that's better," Nicopolis said. "You were hanging too high. I wouldn't want you to miss a moment of this." He waved a hand at the figure crumbled in the mud. "You might want to say your final farewell before he melts." Cackling, he stepped back and walked over to the Lightbringers congratulating each other. He beckoned to the blonde giant. "Occam, take the rest and see if our brothers need any assistance, especially with Sukalli."

"What about you?" Occam asked.

"Once I'm finished here, I'll rendezvous with you at the lodge."

The Lightbringers vanished in a blast of wind. Clasping his hands behind him, Nicopolis began strolling around Basil's body, pausing to give it a kick every now and then. "I've always wondered just how long it takes to return to our Elements. Perhaps we should time him for future reference." He peered at his wristwatch, then beamed up at Griffin. "I have a feeling I'm going to be doing this a great deal more in the coming days." He kicked the body again, harder.

Rage flooded Griffin. "Don't you touch him," he rasped, spitting the words out.

"Or what?" He lifted his foot.

"Or I will bloody kill you."

"*I will bloody kill you,*" Nicopolis mocked. "Why, you sound just like your Mentor."

"That's right." An idea whisked through Griffin's mind. "Which is why you're afraid of me. Just like you were afraid of him."

Nicopolis snorted. "Afraid? Of you? Oh, I think you have that reversed." He sauntered closer. "I can keep you hanging there for days suffering from lack of water and food." He grabbed the Tiro's chin, his nails digging in. "Rather like old times."

Griffin spat in his face.

Again.

Nicopolis stood frozen in shock. Then, in a scream of

fury, he grabbed Griffin by the throat and tore him from the rock.

Free to move, Griffin flung himself on his enemy. Leading with a shoulder and driving with his legs in a move Nan-ja had shown him, he forced Nicopolis back on his heels. When the ex-Mentor flung out his arms for balance, Griffin snatched at the *arba'a*. Catching hold of the chain, he yanked, trying to snap it.

"Oh, no, you don't!" Nicopolis wrapped his fingers around the *arba'a*. His other hand clutched Griffin's wrist.

Locked together, they staggered across the clearing, almost nose-to-nose. Agony crept up his wrist when the ex-Mentor began squeezing the bones, grinding them together. Spinning about in an effort to break each other's hold, they tripped over Basil's body and crashed to the ground in a tangle of arms and legs. The chain sliced Griffin's fingers as it was wrenched from his grasp.

With a surge of *arba'a*-enhanced Might, Nicopolis flipped Griffin onto his back. Pinning him down, and with one hand still holding the *arba'a*, he slapped his free hand against the Tiro's chest. He leaned closer.

"I cannot tell you," he said, lips curled back from yellow teeth. "How much pleasure it brings me to kill the two of you within minutes of each other." With a snarl, he pushed harder.

Griffin cried out. His body seemed to rip apart, joint by joint. Shadowy rings encircled the edge of his vision. They grew larger until only a pinprick of light was left.

Then the light vanished.

Darkness.

The pain faded. An eternity passed.

Then another one.

Griffin waited. Then, mentally, he scratched his head.

So...so am I dead? Funny. I don't feel *dead. But maybe this is what being dead feels like. But would I be able to* think *about being dead if I was dead? It feels like I'm dead-but-not-dead.*

Still speculating, he became aware of himself floating. There was no up or down. No weight. And amazingly, no fear. For a moment, he thought he was back on the rubber raft in the pond, the sun warm on bare skin as he drifted along; the breeze wafting over him scented with pine and earth and the melting snow from the faraway peaks.

Maybe Basil was *right. Death is nothing to be afraid of.* Hope flickered like a candle flame. *Hey, maybe* he's *here, too. In this dead-not-dead state.*

Basil? It's me. Griffin.

No answer.

Before he could try again, an odd humming began to sing through his body. He could feel the vibration of each note. They tingled along his skin and even to the ends of his hair. The floating sensation intensified.

Then, rising up like a choir on an Easter morning, the humming increased. He rose along with it. It ended in an almighty shout. With a grunt, he crashed back to the ground, mud spraying up from the impact.

He opened his eyes and gasped.

Light exploded from within him. It burst out of his open mouth in a deep roar and fractured into a million tiny points of brightness; they began careening about like shooting stars, frenetic with purpose.

Standing nearby, Nicopolis swatted at the sparks dive-bombing him. He spun about, waving an arm like a man being attacked by a swarm of bees. One of the Lights banked around him, picked up speed, and came in for the kill. The ex-Mentor screamed when it bore through his hand still clutching the *arba'a* and into his chest. With a *pop*, it came out his back. He fell away from Griffin in a heap. Smoke trickled out of both holes.

Struggling to his knees, Griffin swiveled his head, trying to follow the action. One point of Light ruffled his hair as it zoomed past and skipped across Basil. The force of its momentum rolled the Mentor's body onto its back. Then, gathering together into a cloud, the Lights hovered overhead, casting a glow on the angels. An odd silence filled the clearing.

Gazing at his Mentor's motionless features, Griffin crouched in the mud, unable to move or even think. It seemed as if a door had quietly closed in his face, just as he was about to step through, leaving him outside in the cold. Alone in the world.

"Oh, Basil," he whispered through numb lips. "What do I do now?"

One of the Lights flew closer. A voice whispered from within the brilliance. "Why, ask, young one."

Griffin blinked. "W-what?"

"Ask. And it shall be given," the voice said again.

If he hadn't been already kneeling, Griffin would have dropped to his knees. Even so, he bowed his head. Before he could form the words, to plead for the impossible, the Light flared. It shot up, ricocheted off the cliff face, and dove down into Basil.

Nothing happened.

Then Basil sighed softly as if awakening. His chest rose and fell and rose again.

Griffin could have watched its movement forever. But when his Mentor lifted a hand, reaching for something, he scrambled closer. He grabbed the searching hand and squeezed it tight.

"Basil?" he whispered. He held his breath and waited.

"Fin." The name ghosted between Basil's lips. His right eye fluttered open. He blinked a few times. "Am I dead?"

Griffin half laughed, half sobbed as he shook his head. "Not anymore."

"Are you quite certain?"

"Yes, sir."

Radiance flicked over their heads. They looked up. The sparks began swirling like fireflies on a summer evening. As they watched in wonder, the Lights disappeared into the fog.

"What are those things?"

"I'm not certain, lad."

Gripping Griffin's arm for support, Basil pulled himself into a sitting position. "What happened?" After the Tiro gave a brief account, he looked about. "And where's Nicopolis now?"

"Over there. He got nailed by one of those Tinkerbells," Griffin joked. Joy and gratitude made him want to fly up or bow down. He wasn't sure which. Maybe both.

With Griffin's help, Basil staggered over to the motionless figure. He reached down and pressed his fingers against Nicopolis' throat. "He's dead."

"We should drive a wooden stake through his heart. Just in case."

"Oh, I don't think that will be necessary." Basil pointed toward a blackened hole in the center of the dead angel's chest. Next to him, the *arba'a* lay broken into two pieces.

"Did the Light do that?"

"No, Fin, I think *you* did. In a way. Of course, I'll need to confirm my theory with Mayla."

"What theory? What are you talking about?"

"Do you recall what Sukalli told us? If the power of the *arba'a* is used to harm a mortal, its power rebounds on the wearer and kills him instead."

"But I'm not a human anymore." Griffin stiffened and glanced down at himself. "Am I?" With a look of panic, he snapped his fingers. Flames sprouted on their tips. "Whew! You had me worried there for a second."

"You may not be a mortal now, but it appears that you might have retained a trace of humanity. It saved you."

"And destroyed *him*." Griffin shook his head in disbelief. "Now, that's karma."

"True that."

Griffin laughed at the expression coming out of his Mentor's mouth. His eyes widened when he noticed their shadows on the ground. Around them, the rain slowed, then stopped. The fog began to lift. A watery sun gleamed overhead, growing brighter with each minute.

"I sure hope the others are okay," Griffin said. "Talk about being out-numbered and out-gunned." They shared a grin at their friends' voices calling as they searched for them.

Basil clapped a hand on Griffin's shoulder. "Do you have enough energy to fly after all this, Tiro? Or will we be hiking back to the lodge?"

"I could ask you the same question. I'm not the one who died." *At least, I don't think I did.*

Basil gave an experimental leap. He staggered a step upon landing. "Ah, yes. I've decided we'll enjoy a gentle stroll back."

Leaving the cliff wall, they headed through the trees, Griffin helping his still wobbly Mentor over fallen logs. The last of the clouds melted away as the mid-morning sun warmed the air. After a slow half hour, they stepped out of the woods and gazed down the valley.

Four figures clustered near the pond, one sitting on the ground. Basil let loose a sharp whistle. He waved when Sukalli whirled around. The Guardian returned

239

the gesture, relief apparent even from that distance.

"I can't believe it's finally over. And he's really dead." Griffin remarked as they hiked side by side through the wet grass. "I thought I'd feel different, somehow. But I just feel like *me*."

"He has haunted you all your life, Fin. It may take some time for you to adjust to the fact that that particular threat is gone."

They drew nearer to the pond. Griffin broke into a jog when Sergei and Vassar rushed to greet him. Vassar's red hair unfurled behind her as she ran toward him with Sergei on her heels. Without warning, she flung her arms around his neck and kissed him on the cheek.

"I hope you aren't expecting that from me," Sergei said. "Because I don't like you *that* much."

Sukalli and Nan-ja joined them. She paused in front of Griffin and inspected him from head to toe. "I'm happy to see you all in one piece. Are you all right?"

"Yes, ma'am."

"And Nicopolis?" Sukalli asked.

"Dead. By his own hand," Basil said, coming up behind Griffin.

"Good. Saves me the trouble of stringing up a rope," the Guardian said. "And since the others have skedaddled out of here, I reckon we won this skirmish."

"Yeah, but at what price?" Nan-ja said, gazing at Basil. She reached up and touched his face. She smiled when Basil took her hand and kissed it, then kept it in his. Griffin and Vassar shifted their feet, careful to look anywhere, but at the two Mentors.

"You know you're freaking your apprentices, don't you," Sergei said. He shrugged when they glared at him. "I'm just saying."

"They better get use to it," Nan-ja said. She and Basil headed hand-in-hand to the lodge.

The three youths watched for a moment. Then, Sergei offered his arm to Vassar.

She hesitated. "Well, just this once." As they strolled after the Mentors, she glanced back. "Coming, Griffin?"

"He'll be along in a minute." Sukalli waved them away before turning to the Tiro. "I want to talk with you."

"About what?"

"Just something I want to get off my chest. I want to apologize for helping Mayla turn you mortal." Squinting, he followed a hawk as it floated past on outspread wings, its tail a flash of red against the blue sky. "And for not keeping a closer eye on Nicopolis during your early years with him."

Not sure what to say, Griffin nodded. A sudden thought flashed through his mind. "Um...Guardian Sukalli—"

"Ah, heck, just call me Sukalli when Basil's not around. Or even when he is. It would be good for him to lose some of the stiff, upper-lip Brit thing he's got going."

Griffin grinned. "Okay, I'll try to remember."

"Now, what were you going to ask me?"

"Basil mentioned he had a chance to be a Guardian, but he turned it down. Do you know why?"

"Yup."

"Why?"

"Because three years ago, you needed a Mentor. And a home. And a chance."

"Those don't seem like very good reasons."

"Why, pup, they're the best reasons of all."

Chapter Twenty-Nine

"Basil?"

The Mentor looked up from the wooden rocker on the front porch of the lodge. In his hands, a mug of coffee steamed in the mid-morning air. He smiled up at Griffin and Vassar as they stepped out the door and joined him.

"Fin."

"I know you wanted us to take it easy and recuperate. But it's been two days since the fight, and we're all healing pretty well. So, can Vassar and I take the Jeep into town instead of flying?" Griffin grinned proudly. "And I hope you noticed I said *I*, not *me*."

"May I."

"Excuse me?"

"*May* Vassar and I take the Jeep? Not *can* Vassar and I take—"

Vassar burst out laughing. "Told you. Now pay up," she said, holding out a hand. After Griffin forked over a dollar bill, she tucked into the pocket of her orange hoodie.

Basil stood up and fished the keys out of his pocket.

Holding them out of reach, he waited until he had Griffin's attention. "Buckskin Gulch may be a small mountain town, but do try to stay out of trouble."

"What trouble? All it has is one main street, a couple of stores, and a gas station."

"Then why bother to go at all?"

"Because..." Griffin's voice faded as he tried to think of an excuse. He looked at Vassar for help.

"Because they're teenagers," Sergei drawled as he sauntered out the door. "Don't worry. I'll go along and play babysitter." He plucked the keys from Basil's fingers and headed for the vehicle.

"Yeah, like you're sooo much older than us." Vassar jogged after him, her braid swinging back and forth. She clambered in the passenger side as Sergei held the door open for her.

Griffin started after them. He groaned in frustration when Basil snagged his elbow. "Aw, come on, Basil," he snapped, spinning around and glaring up at the Mentor. "Stop with the all the lectures to be careful, to be polite, to look both ways before picking my nose." He flung out his arms. "You do this practically every time I leave the house and I'm getting sick of it. Nan-ja doesn't do it to Vassar. Fire, I'm not some first year apprentice, you know." He huffed out a breath and waited.

"Are you quite through?"

"I guess."

"Then, would you please pick up a dozen eggs from the market? We've run out."

Griffin opened and shut his mouth. "T-that's all you were going to say?"

"Simply that."

"Oh."

Without another word, Griffin jumped off the porch and hurried to the car. Slamming the door behind him, he leaned forward between the seats. "Go, Sergei, before I make a bigger fool out of myself."

"Not possible, dude," Sergei said, shifting into reverse.

Half an hour later, they pulled over and parked the vehicle in front of a small grocery store. Vassar jumped out before either Griffin or Sergei could help her.

"Oh, cool," she said, stomping a foot. "Wooden sidewalks."

Griffin joined her. "So where to first?"

"Listen, you two take off." Sergei craned his neck as he glanced along the street. He tossed the keys to Griffin. "If I'm not here in an hour, then go ahead and drive back to the lodge. I'll fly."

"Why?" Vassar asked. "What are you going to do?"

"None of your business." He started down the sidewalk.

The Tiros glanced at each other, then hurried after him. Their feet made hollow clumping sounds as they strolled along. After passing several storefronts, Sergei halted in front of a narrow building with two large windows blacked out. A neon sign flashed *open* in one of them. On the plain door, a hand lettered wooden sign read *Gotta' Inkling Tattoos. Walk-ins welcome.*

"No freaking way." Vassar's lips curved into a faint smile. "Are you really?"

"I am." Sergei cut his eyes at Griffin. "What do you say—still want one?"

Griffin licked his lips. "Why? Are you scared to go in there by yourself?" he said, stalling for time.

"Basil will kill you," Vassar pointed out. She studied the door with a look of intrigue.

"Yeah, and so would Nan-ja if you did." Griffin's face brightened. "But, hey, there's safety in numbers."

"I will if you will," she said.

Griffin sucked in a deep breath. "Let's do it."

Without another word, the three pushed the door open and stepped inside.

* * *

"What's wrong?" Basil asked at Nan-ja's frown.

Leaning over the railing of the porch, she peered down the road winding through the aspens. "You would think they would have run out of things to do. It's not that big a town."

"Mother hen." He held his book up higher, head turned slightly as he read one-eyed. "Most likely, they stayed in town for lunch."

Hoisting herself up on the railing, Nan-ja swung her foot. "Did I tell you that you look rakish with that black eye patch?"

"*Rakish*? I've been called many things in my life, but

never rakish."

"Well, the whole pirate thing really fits you for some reason." She laughed when Basil shifted in the rocker, redness heating his face as he adjusted the eye patch.

They both looked down the road at the rumble of an engine. A few minutes later, the Jeep coasted to a stop in a crunch of gravel, Griffin at the wheel. As the Mentors watched, the Tiros climbed out gingerly, as if they were fearful of making any sudden movements. Sergei remained seated in the back.

Griffin walked toward the lodge, a small paper bag in one hand. "Got the eggs." He jogged up the steps and went inside. Vassar stayed behind.

"Did you have a good time?" Nan-ja asked as Vassar climbed up next to her on the railing.

"Yeah, it was okay. Not much to do. We got some snacks and just walked around."

"Why is Sergei still in the Jeep?" Basil asked.

"Oh, he wasn't feeling good on the way back," Griffin said as he reemerged from the lodge. "Hey, Sergei," he yelled toward the vehicle. "Want some help?"

The back door swung open. Sergei crawled out, face as pale as his hair. Clutching the doorframe in a white-knuckle grip, he started to stand, then slumped back down, a greenish tinge around his mouth.

"Motion sick?" Nan-ja guessed.

"Something like that." Vassar smiled at Griffin, who grinned back. "We better go help him before he throws up." They headed over.

"They're up to something," Basil remarked. "I can tell."

Nan-ja snorted. "Gee, you think?"

* * *

Reaching Sergei, Griffin and Vassar each grabbed an arm and eased him upright. He swayed for a moment before catching his balance.

"Still hurting?" Vassar whispered. She kept a hand on his arm.

"It's not the pain," Sergei said hoarsely. "It was the sight of that needle. Every time I think about it, I want to throw up." He sucked in a deep breath and pulled free. "And stop hovering—you're going to make the Mentors suspicious." Straightening with an effort, Sergei led the way to the lodge. Griffin and Vassar flanked him on either side.

"That's what I get for letting Junior here drive," Sergei announced loudly as he climbed the steps. "I think I'll go upstairs and lay down for a while until my stomach stops trying to join us." He disappeared inside.

"What a wimp." Griffin caught Vassar's eye. "I'm starving—want to go raid the kitchen?" He stepped to one side, allowing her to enter first.

Once inside, they hurried past the stone fireplace; a crack snaked up along one side of it, weaving between various boulders before disappearing into the ceiling. Tiptoeing up the stairs as quietly as they could, they scurried along the hall to Vassar's room and darted inside, leaving the door open.

"How's it feeling?" she asked.

"It's still a little tender, but not too bad. You did a good job. How about yours?"

"Fair. I *could* use one more shot of Might-healing if you're up for it." She plopped on the bed. Rolling up her pant leg, she revealed an ankle tattooed with a small red flame. "And stop saying you suck at it."

With a look of doubt, Griffin squatted down and laid a hand on her ankle. He was surprised how delicate it felt; he could almost wrap his fingers around it. Her skin was warm, but not as tanned as his.

Closing his eyes, he focused. Might swelled like a balloon in the middle of his chest. He imagined it flowing down his arm and out of his fingers. He scrunched his face tighter.

"Uh, I think you got it," Vassar said a moment later, a hint of amusement in her voice.

His eyes flew open. "Right." He let go and stood up. "How's that?"

She wiggled her foot. "Nice. Now, my turn."

Griffin hesitated for a moment. Feeling his face reddening, he turned around and pulled his tee shirt up. He swallowed when Vassar pushed it higher to expose his right shoulder blade.

"I can see why you changed your mind about the double tattoos," Vassar said as she laid her palm on his back. "I like the griffin symbol better, especially in this dark green color." Soothing warmth spread from her hand as she worked.

"Griffin is a Welsh name," he blurted out, trying to think about something else other than Vassar's hand on his skin. "It means 'strong in faith.'"

"It fits you. Now, stop talking, so I can concentrate." A minute later, she stepped back. "Wow, I *am* good. It looks almost healed."

"Thanks." He pulled the shirt down. "Are you going to tell Nan-ja about it?"

"Tell me about what?" said a voice from the doorway.

They spun around. Nan-ja stood there, arms folded across her chest. She arched a delicate eyebrow. "Tell me about what?" she repeated.

"Nothing," the Tiros said at the same time.

She snorted. "Try again."

Vassar chewed on her lip as Griffin shifted from foot to foot. Nan-ja dropped her arms and leaned a shoulder against the door frame, waiting.

Vassar broke.

"We...I mean, *I*...got a tattoo."

"No, *we* did," Griffin jumped in. "And it wasn't Vassar's idea. It was mine."

Nan-ja ignored him. She walked into the room. "Let me see it, Vassar." When the Tiro pulled up her pant leg, she bent over and examined it. "Well, I can't say I'm pleased you did this behind my back. But it does look like it's healing cleanly." She straightened up. Vassar quailed when the Mentor tightened her lips. "But next time, Tiro, you check with me before you pull a stunt like that. *Wakarimasu ka?*"

"*Hai*, I understand."

"You got one, too?" Nan-ja turned on Griffin.

"Yes, ma'am."

"Go tell your Mentor."

"Could *you* just yell at me or something?"

She stabbed a thumb over her shoulder. "Move it. I want to speak with Vassar in private anyway."

The door closed with a bang behind Griffin. Dragging his feet, he made his way down the stairs; the sound of running water pulled him toward kitchen. He pushed sideways through the swinging doors. Basil stood at the sink, filling the tea kettle. As Griffin walked in, he placed it on the stove.

"Um, Basil, I have to tell you something."

"Tell me what?"

"Promise not to get mad?"

Basil closed his eye briefly. He waved Griffin over. "Should I be sitting down for this?"

"Uh, I don't think so. But Nan-ja said I had to tell you."

Alarm colored Basil's face. "Nan-ja?"

"Yes, sir. She already knows about Vassar's."

"Vassar's what?"

Griffin mumbled something under his breath.

"I beg your pardon?"

"I *said*, I got a tattoo."

Basil stiffened. "Where?"

"In town."

251

"No, I mean, where on your body?"

"On my shoulder blade."

Basil motioned for him to turn around. "Let me see."

Griffin swallowed and pulled up his shirt. Silence filled the kitchen.

"Well, an appropriate symbol," Basil said after a moment. He leaned back against the counter. "Did they use a single needle?" he asked as Griffin tugged his shirt into place.

"Yes, sir."

"And does it hurt much?"

"Vassar did some Might-healing, so, no. It's just a little sore."

Basil nodded. "Before you get another one, I would like you to speak with me first. Understand?"

"Yes, sir."

"And I take it from Sergei's odd behavior, he got one, too?"

"Yes, sir—a Russian bear." Griffin shook his head. "Who would have thought a needle would freak *him* out."

"Location?"

"Well, let's just say neither Vassar or I wanted to help with Might-healing."

"Ah. No need to elaborate. Please ask Nan-ja if she would like some tea."

Griffin started to leave, then paused. "So I'm not in trouble?"

"No, you are not in trouble. Off you go." Basil made a

shooing gesture with his hand. Before his Mentor could change his mind, Griffin hurried back out of the kitchen.

Okay, that is beyond weird, he thought as he trotted back up the stairs. *Now, why he didn't he get mad? This seems like something he would go all* parental *about.* "Mentors," he said with a shake of his head.

Chapter Thirty

Basil's Journal: Saturday, June 11th

An old enemy destroyed. New friendships begun. And a radical group has been formed who is determined to split the Terrae Angeli apart in a way no one could have foreseen.

All in all, a busy few weeks.

How we will deal with those dissenters is still unknown. Flight Command is torn in two. While a few suggest we devote every Terrae Angelus to stopping the Lightbringers, most realize that we cannot, in good faith, pull that many guardian angels out of the field. Our first mandate is to guard and protect mortals. At whatever the cost to ourselves.

On a lighter note: I know Griffin is still trying to determine why he didn't get in trouble over that tattoo. Frankly, I think it would have been unfair to punish him for getting one.

Since I have one myself.

Griffin's Journal: Saturday, June 11th

Miss Lena once told me that nothing is ever all bad.

That if we search for the good in people or events, we will find it.

She was right.

Take Sergei. I wouldn't say we're friends. Maybe more like allies. Or even brothers. And in spite of him being a jerk most of the time, I know I can count on him to have my back. And Vassar, too.

Vassar. I don't know how I'm supposed to think about her. She's a good friend, I do know that.

I also know she's lucky to have a Mentor like Nan-ja. Talk about cool. Except when she and Basil are making eyes at each other. In front of us. Really, guys?

And Guardian Sukalli. Fire, I used to be so scared of him. But, now I see why he and Basil are such good friends. But, talk about total opposites.

Kind of like me and Sergei.

Chapter Thirty-One

Crouching outside Katie's window, Griffin peered through the glass. The final rays of the setting sun cast his shadow across her bedroom. Spying the door swinging open, he watched with a grin while she tossed a stack of neatly folded clothes onto an older pile on the bed, then cocked her head when she noticed his shadow. She looked up.

For a moment, they stared at each other. Then, Katie flung herself across the room. Grabbing the handle, she cranked it as fast as she could. Before it was fully open, Griffin squeezed through and stepped inside.

Their kiss lasted a long time.

Finally, Griffin drew back, his arms still wrapped around her. "I-I don't know where to start. How to tell you everything that happened."

"That kiss was a pretty good beginning."

They turned their heads at the sound of thundering paws on the stairs. A moment later, Bear burst into the room. With a booming *whoof*, he rushed over to the angel.

Griffin reached down and grabbed the enormous

dog on both sides of his long head. "Hey, big guy!" Bear tried to lick any part of the angel's hands he could reach. "Yeah, I'm glad to see you, too." He ruffled the dog's ears, then pushed him gently away. "Now, where were we?"

"Katie? Did I hear..?" Helen Heflin appeared in the doorway. She smiled with delight. "Griffin! You're home!"

He grinned. "Hi, Mrs. Heflin." His cheeks reddened when she hurried over and gave him a warm hug.

Stepping back, she peered into his face. "I'm guessing by your smile that everything turned out okay. And Basil?"

Griffin hesitated. "Um, he's fine. He said to tell you and Mr. Heflin hello and that he'll stop by tomorrow." Guilt poked at him. *I'll let him explain about his eye. I'm not ready to talk about it.*

Helen nodded. "May I ask about Nicopolis?"

"H-he's dead."

Both mother and daughter gasped. "How?" Katie asked.

"Well, we're not sure yet. Basil is meeting with Guardian Sukalli about what took place. For now, let's just say that the old maxim about karma is true: what goes around, comes around." He glanced out the window. "I've got to get back soon. I was only supposed to come over for a little while and let you know we were home."

"I'll let you two finish saying hello, then," Helen said. "Please tell Basil that Lewis and I will be looking forward to hearing the details." She whistled for Bear and pulled the door closed behind her.

Griffin joined Katie by the window. He sat down on the wide ledge and pulled her onto his lap. Wrapping arms around her, he held her for a moment, breathing in the vanilla scent of her shampoo. "I missed you."

"Me, too. It feels like forever since we were together." She snuggled closer. "So, he's really gone? Can you give me more details?"

After Griffin finished telling his story, he added, "and not only did I get that wacko out of my life, I think Sergei and I are finally..."

"Friends?"

"Well, at least, not enemies. More like allies."

"And Vassar?"

"Vassar is like a sister to me. Even if she can kick my butt during drills."

"Good."

"Good like she's a sister or that she can kick my butt?"

"Both."

They laughed, then Griffin asked. "And what's new with Cas?" he asked, careful to keep his voice neutral.

"Nice try acting like you're not jealous, Angel Boy." She grinned when he protested his innocence. "Come on! Cas is a friend. A really good friend. To both of us."

"Just checking. Listen, I better get back."

They both stood up. After another lingering kiss, Griffin climbed out the window, took a quick glance around, then disappeared. Landing by his own open window, he gave a final wave and slipped inside.

At that moment, Sergei sauntered in. "Hey. I'm taking off."

Griffin walked around the bed and began pulling dirty clothes out his duffle bag. "Already?" He sniffed a still damp tee shirt and threw it toward the laundry basket in the corner.

"Yeah, well. Mission accomplished and all that. Plus, I never got a chance to unpack my stuff over at my new apartment."

"Oh. Right." Griffin hesitated for a moment before sticking out his hand. "So, um, thanks. For saving my life. Twice."

"Three times, but who's counting?" Sergei grinned as they shook hands. "See you around High Springs." He grabbed his bag sitting by the door and left. Griffin listened as Sergei called a farewell to Basil. The front door opened and closed a minute later.

After emptying his bag, he grabbed the overflowing basket and headed downstairs with it. Leaving it in the tiny laundry room tucked under the stairs, he continued on to the kitchen. He opened the refrigerator and made a face.

"Hey, Basil?" he yelled. "There's nothing to eat."

"Have you looked in the freezer," the Mentor called back from the study.

Griffin checked. "Nothing but half a bag of frozen onion rings."

"Ring for take out, then."

"Pizza or Chinese?"

"Both," Sukalli boomed. "Then come talk with us, little brother."

After placing both orders, Griffin headed through the living room to Basil's study. He took a seat next to the Guardian on the sofa. "Okay, pizza will probably get here first. I ordered vegetarian everything, so we're all good to go."

Basil nodded, distracted, as he bent over an ancient book at the desk. The thin pages rustled when he turned them. For several minutes, the only sound was the crackling of paper and scratch of the Mentor's pen as he took notes on a legal pad.

"Well, that would explain a great deal." Basil sat back and picked up the notes. "Mayla was correct about the *arba'a* destroying the Terrae Angelus who misuses its powers. And her comment about karma was prescient. By first being the cause of Fin's temporary mortality, and later, by trying to kill him with the *arba'a*, Nicopolis brought about his own destruction."

"I think that's called irony," Griffin pointed out. "What?" he added at Basil's expression. "Hey, I learned *something* from my English class." A question flashed through his mind. "By the way, what about the other Lightbringers. Did they get away?"

"They vamoosed right after Nicopolis died," Sukalli said. "I guess that young one...what was his name?"

"Wilhelm," Griffin supplied.

Sukalli blinked. "You're pulling my leg. *Wilhelm?*"

"How Teutonic," Basil murmured.

"As I was saying," Sukalli continued. "That young one must have been hanging around in secret, watching the three of you. I'm guessing that when he saw Nicopolis bite the dust, he hightailed it over to his compadres and informed them. Which was lucky for us, because we couldn't have held out much longer."

The iron doorknocker rapped twice. "Goodness, that was quick." Basil pulled out his wallet and handed some bills to Griffin. "Don't forget to tip them."

Griffin opened the door at the second knock. Nan-ja and Vassar stood there, balancing four boxes of pizza. The aroma of cheese and garlic filled the entry way. Behind them, a delivery van was pulling away from the curb.

"Here." Nan-ja handed him the boxes before he could say anything. "We paid the guy already. Make yourself useful and carry them on back to the kitchen. Vassar, go with him. We'll be along directly." She walked past them into Basil's study and closed the door behind her.

"What's going on?" Griffin asked as he led the way through the living room to the kitchen. Behind him, Vassar looked around in curiosity.

"I don't know. When we got home this evening, Guardian Mayla was waiting for us. Nan-ja and she talked in private for about half an hour, then she left. Right afterwards, we came straight here. I bugged her all the way

here, but she said she wanted to meet with Basil and Sukalli first."

They piled the boxes on the kitchen table. Opening
the top one, he gestured for Vassar to help herself, then
he freed a slice from its cheesy leash and took a bite. Still
chewing, he looked up when the Mentors and Sukalli
walked in. The Guardian was speaking on his cell phone;
he put it away as everyone took a seat.

"Well?" Griffin asked around a mouthful.

Sukalli grabbed a slice for himself. "Looks like Nicopolis' followers are still determined to go through with this
brave new world order of theirs. Occam is leading them
now. So Flight Command has come up with a strategy."

"I still say it's too dangerous for the Tiros," Basil argued. "After all, the Lightbringers still have their *arba'as*."

"What's too dangerous?" Griffin and Vassar asked at
the same time.

"Command wants a posse of Terrae Angeli to hunt
them down. We'll be packing a formal mandate to do
whatever is necessary to stop those renegades."

"We?" With a look of hope, Griffin started to ask when
the back door opened. Sergei strolled in; his still unpacked
bag over one shoulder.

"Got your message half way home, Sukalli. What's going on?" he asked, dumping the pack in the corner. Taking
a seat next to Vassar, he helped himself to the pizza.

"We're got orders to go after the rest of the Lightbringers," Sukalli said. "I'm putting together a strike force."

"You can count me in—those guys are giving us Wind

and Waters a bad rap. Not that we don't deserve it once in a while," Sergei said with a cocky grin.

All eyes turned toward the Mentors. Basil and Nan-ja looked at each. A silent question was asked, then answered. Both Tiros sat up straight and held their breaths.

"Well, Vassar and I are coming along," Nan-ja said. She shook her head at her Tiro's cheer. "After all, you guys are going to need all the help you can get."

Almost afraid to ask, Griffin looked at Basil, who hesitated, adjusting his eye patch. Relief flooded him when the Mentor finally nodded.

"'We band of brothers,' eh?" Basil smiled when Griffin pumped a fist into the air. "Speaking metaphorically," he quickly added as Nan-ja raised an eyebrow.

"Guess we got our team, then." Sukalli reached for another slice. "We better start making plans—"

A knock echoed through the house.

"I'll get it. It's probably the Chinese food." Griffin rose to his feet. Heading toward the front door, he fished in his pocket for the money Basil had given him earlier. Halfway across the living room, he slammed to a stop.

Oh, crap! What I am going to tell Katie? She's going to freak when she learns I'm taking off again. After a moment, he shook his head. *Nah, it'll be okay—she'll understand. I hope.* A second knock moved his feet.

The delivery girl stood there, nervously snapping her gum. She did a double take when she saw Griffin. An approving look spread across her face. "Hi there. Here's your order." The aroma of ginger sauce and steamed broccoli rose from the pair of plastic bags. "That will be fifty-two, seventy-six. I think. It's my first night on the job." She studied him, twirling a lock of hair around a finger while she waited for him to count out the money. "So, do you go to school around here?"

"Not anymore."

"Oh, have you graduated?"

"I'm only sixteen."

"Home schooled?"

"Nope, not really. But—" He paused to hand her the money. "—can you keep a secret?"

She giggled. "Sure."

Griffin glanced around, then spoke in a conspiratorial tone. "I'm an angel."

"W-what?"

Making sure he raised his voice so that it carried to the back of the house, he repeated. "I said *I'm an angel.*"

"I heard that, Griffin!"

He grinned at Basil's roar of frustration from the kitchen, then yelled over a shoulder. "My dad's an angel, too!"

"GRIFFIN!"

Laughing, he leaned closer to the bewildered girl. "But I'm not supposed to tell anyone about us," he whispered.

"I-I-I have to go," the girl stammered as she backed away. When she reached a safe distance, she turned and sprinted down the driveway. A moment later, the car screeched away from curb leaving behind the stink of burnt rubber.

"It never gets old." Digging in one of the bags for a preemptive snack, Griffin pulled out a spring roll and stepped out onto the porch. He leaned a shoulder against one of the post. Munching, he studied Katie's darkened window through the falling dusk.

He sighed as he remembered the first time he had flown to her window. The night before his Proelium. *It seems like a million years ago*, he thought. *So much has happened since then; I can't even wrap my head around it all. Angel to mortal to angel again. Even though she never really said it, I know Katie wanted me to stay human. And a tiny part of me wishes I still was, for her sake. Why, I bet Mayla could change me back again, and probably even find a way to make it permanent.*

The twinkle of the first star of the evening caught his eye. He looked up. *But, I'm pretty sure He wanted me to be this. So this I shall stay. I'll just have to figure out the rest of it as I go along.*

Basil called out, asking what was taking so bloody long. Griffin glanced one last time across the street, then headed back inside to join the other angels.

Author's Note

As I've mentioned in my two previous books, *Griffin Rising* and *Griffin's Fire*, it was in the summer of 2009 that I came across an obscure and rather brief description from the Middle Ages about a lower caste of angels. According to Catholic tradition, these angels, besides acting as guardians of humankind, were also said to control the four elements of earth, fire, wind, and water. And thus, Griffin, Basil, and the other Terrae Angeli were born.

Elaborating on the idea of an angelic chain of command, the fictitious Kellsfarne Manuscript gives a nod to the early Christian writing *The Celestial Hierarchy*, which is a work from the fifth century that influenced Thomas Aquinas, a medieval Catholic priest and theologian who divided angels into a pecking order, so to speak, based on their proximity to God.

However, the belief in supernatural or angelic beings can be found in many of the world's religions and is not limited to Christianity. I borrowed from Judaism as well as Islam, Hinduism, and ancient Babylon; for example, *Sukalli* is a Babylonian term meaning *angel* or *messenger*. And to emphasize the antiquity of the Terrae Angeli, I used the Latin phrase, *Tiro*, as a synonym for *apprentice* or *young recruit* just as *Proelium* is Latin for *battle*.

In addition to religious influences, I've also added bits and pieces from other cultures and historical events. Touches of classical Sparta, the Irish myths of Cuchulainn and the Red Branch, the European feudal system, the Plains Indians of North America, and Great Britain's Royal Air Force during World War Two all found their way into Griffin's tale.

In this third book of the series, part of my inspiration came from William Shakespeare. His play, *Henry V*, contains a speech in which the English king, Henry, bolsters the courage of his outnumbered men by reminding them that 'the fewer men, the greater share of honour,' and that a small 'band of brothers' can prevail against overwhelming evil as well as overwhelming odds.

And, in Chapter Twelve, Basil recited one of my favorite verses from the Bible: Ephesians, chapter 6, verse 12. A fitting passage for these warriors of Heaven.

With the Lightbringers' borderline racial hatred of Earth and Fire angels, I reached back in time to both the Nazi party pogroms against the Jews as well as the centuries of racial discrimination in the United States. Sadly, these ugly blots on humankind's history seem to have spilled over into the angelic realm.

And the Orphan Boy Mine is indeed a real abandoned gold mine. It sits halfway up the valley from my humble vacation cabin in the Colorado Rockies. Many a time I have mountain-biked past its entrance, studying the tailings and wondering if I could find a way to work its name and location into one of my books.

I guess I can check *that* off my to-do list.

Acknowledgements

Once again, I wish to thank my family and friends for sticking with me through another book, especially my mother, Mary Louise Maes. She has always been my first and finest beta reader. See, Mom? I *told* you Griffin would be okay. And, no, I would never kill off Basil.

I would also like to thank Kaci Guthrie M.Ed., who patiently allowed me to blather on about my characters. All. The. Time. She is the consummate bibliophile and her passion for books makes her library a magic place for teens.

But I owe the greatest debt to my editor, Todd "Thor" Craig. Like the Norse deity, he hammered my manuscript into a better book and would not let me settle for less than god-like perfection.

Thanks, also, to the Cheyenne Mountain Junior High Book Club of 2012-2013 for allowing me to share Griffin with them.

And for all the fans, Bev, Kelly, Tracy (smiley face), Carmel, Brooke (Brookster!), Cait, Savannah, Jenny, Naj, Marcie, Leisha, Kathy, Kate, Carrie, Lynn, Stephanie, Amy, Lori, Greg, Tiffany, Ashley, Beth, Katie, and Jan, this one is for you.

Thanks for keeping the faith that Nicopolis will be defeated, Griffin will be victorious, and Basil will always be Basil.

About the Author

All her life, the archetypal hero and his journey have enthralled Darby Karchut. A native of New Mexico, Darby grew up in a family that venerated books and she spent her childhood devouring one fantasy novel after another. Fascinated by mythologies from around the world, she attended the University of New Mexico, graduating with a degree in anthropology. After moving to Colorado, she then earned a master's in education and became a social studies teacher.

Drawing from her extensive knowledge of world cultures, she blends ancient myths with modern urban life to write stories that relate to young teens today.

Darby is a member of the Society of Children's Book Writers and Illustrators and the Pikes Peak Writers Guild. She lives in Colorado Springs, Colorado with her husband, which is the setting of both her series. When not writing or teaching at a local junior high school, she enjoys running, biking, and skiing the Rocky Mountains in all types of weather.

Her other books include *Griffin Rising* (the 2011 Sharp Writ YA Book of the Year) and *Griffin's Fire* (the 2012 Readers Favorite Bronze Medal Award Winner) as well as a new series for younger teens, *Finn Finnegan* (Spencer Hill Press, March 2013) based on Celtic mythology.

Visit the author at www.darbykarchut.com